Career Suicide Comes in Twelve Colors

Collected Stories 2010-2021 by Izaak David Diggs

© 2021 Izaak David Diggs
ISBN 978-1-7345428-8-2
Cover by Ike James
Released Halloween 2021

das flob das flob das flob das flob das flob das flob das flob das flob das flob das flob

das flob das flob das flob das flob The Raft das flob das flob das flob

das flob das flob das flob das flob das flob das flob das flob das flob das flob das flob das flob das flob das flob das flob

1

"David Myer!"

A man's voice was echoing down the canyon, almost sing-song. Laughing.

My friends looked at me. The raft was drifting towards the shallows but the others didn't seem to notice.

"David Myer!"

I thought that I had pinpointed where the voice was coming from but there was no one there. My friends were staring at me, openly suspicious.

Dudes...I have no idea why whatever this is knows my name.

I didn't say that, though; they wouldn't have believed me. Why should they? The Invisible Man knew my name.

"I think he's up on that cliff." Ben, looking up at the same spot I was.

"There's nothing up there." Lee: Contempt and other forms of hostility.

"The Invisible Man knows you." Marcus had picked up on the fact that we were running aground and worked his oar to push us out of the shallows.

"I honestly have no idea why," Me, working my own oar.

Lee paddled through her disgust. Her muscles were getting sunburned.

Ben did not row. He was looking up at the cliff where the voice seemed to be coming from. My friend was sitting back as if the end of the raft were a couch, looking calm or at least thoughtful.

"Did I tell you guys when I took too many mushrooms at Burningman?" He asked softly.

"Yes---" I replied.

"What the fuck does that have to do with anything?" Lee, at least she was turning her anger on someone else.

Ben remained calm and nodded in the direction of the Invisible Man

"Something was talking to me, a voice like the Invisible Man," he continued.

"So...David is on mushrooms or this is all a flashback of yours?" Marcus asked.

It was easy to tell that he was getting irritated as well. Ben did not seem to notice, he even closed his eyes.

"The voice told me I had to go back to find the answer," he said.

Ben's eyes opened and focused on me. Was *I* supposed to answer?

"Go back? Go back to *when*?" I asked.

"No, go back to *what*," Ben replied with a grin equally sly and beatific.

Now all three of them were staring at me, expecting some resolution to all the weird shit that had been happening since we dropped the raft in the water.

"Okay…let's do something simple," Ben continued, picking up his oar but using it as a baton. "Tell me how this story starts."

"You mean our raft trip?" I asked.

"Yes, but your part of it. Do you remember how it started?"

"What the fuck does this have to do with anything?" Lee, under her breath.

"You mean the day I got your email?"

"Yeah," Ben smiled, happier than he had any right to be. "Go back to that."

2

Yeah...go back to that.

That morning I had the dream again:

I'm sitting on the couch. Angela is sitting close as she talks with her parents. She begins playing with my hair, I close my eyes. There is the sensation of my scalp being pulled so I open my eyes and look over at her. Angela looks confused and sets the phone down.

"Did you get stitches?"

"When I was a kid. I think I remember them being removed--"

Her hand makes a pinching shape that disappears behind my left eye. The tugging starts again, becomes painful.

"Hey---maybe we should just leave it," I say through gritted teeth.

"Relax. I'm getting it."

A feeling like a paper cut and then she is holding a piece of black string maybe six inches in length. Blood is dripping off the lower end. It drips onto Angela's jeans but she doesn't notice.

"Weird..."

And then the string begins to twitch.

Cut to: Me lying in bed awake, anxious---the dream has always been a portent of something big: Grandmother dying. The doctor telling me that my recovery was complete. Angela and I separating. And there it was again.

The beginning of this story goes like this.

3

"You fucking knew," Lee setting her oar down to get a beer.

"Come on, let's remember we're friends." Marcus, shooting me a dirty look none-the-less.

"You had the dream before the invite and you didn't tell us?"

"Dav-id M-yer!" The Invisible Man laughs after he calls out; I can feel his laughter on my skin. It stays there like a film.

There are more rocks. The current becomes angry, an argument of water; all of us have to work the oars. The discussion is forgotten until we are back in calm water.

"You should have warned us that you had the dream," Marcus, pursing his lips.

"It's just a dream," I say, more defensive than I intended. "Come on, we're too old for believing---"

"Something always happens!" Lee, yelling. Her anger echoes off the canyon walls. "Every time for the last twenty-five years you've had the stitch dream shit happens."

"Good stuff sometimes." Me, meekly, ashamed. Why should I be? Why? But, yes, I feel ashamed.

"You need to keep going," Ben says, the only one of us remotely serene. I look at him, he nods.

"You mean, with what happened that morning?"

"Yeah."

"Why? All you guys think *this* is because I had the dream."

Defensive? Can you blame me?

"There's always something more." Ben reaches for his pipe, lights it.

4

I had the dream with Angela pulling the stitch, that much is still vivid. From there it's a guess, examining my usual routines: After waking up, it was time to move the truck.

That was my routine when I woke up; moving the truck and parking it near my favorite coffee shop. There was this barista that fascinated me. Her eyes were so pale blue they were nearly translucent...

She was a kid so there was no hitting on her or anything like that. Cue: Middle aged man taking his coffee cup with a polite nod.

That was my place to wake up, do all my on-line stuff, and use the toilet. I was between work assignments so there was time to dwell on pale blue eyes, go on long walks, and try and figure out getting the money to live.

Did Ben's email come in the same morning as the dream? Probably. The more that question is turned over and over more details come back and the answer is...probably.

I can see it, the little depiction of an envelope telling me to check my inbox---I had not been expecting Ben to write me.

It was even more of a surprise that included in his message was an invitation to go rafting with him and the others.

I didn't answer right away; partly because my brain had yet to form a reply but also because there was a desire to not come across as too *eager*.

Thank God you wrote. I am so sorry, it was all my fault we argued. Yes, I will come along, I will do whatever if we can just be friends again.

You see the problem with a hasty reply, right?

When the coffee cup was just a couple of drops on the bottom I bussed my table and went to the bathroom. I sat on the toilet. A minute later the barista broke in. She looked at me coyly then locked the door before unbuttoning her work shirt. Only a thin strappy sort of white slip was underneath. Her nipples were visible through the fabric. The barista removed her pants, unzipped mine, and pulled my penis out.

"I like your cock---"

Someone dropped something heavy outside the bathroom door and she was gone. Probably for the best, I've never been comfortable jerking off in a public restroom; it always feels weird with all the conversations and then there's my phobia that I've left the door unlocked.

I walked out a few minutes later. The barista was helping other customers. Friendly girl, probably just a nice decent person--- Unlike me. Jesus; what was she? Twenty-two? Younger? If she knew what lechery went on in my head...

And I see why I find her beautiful; she looks like a younger Angela...

My ex wife. Lying on the bed asleep. But she wasn't asleep, was she?

Emotions were coming on in public, I needed to leave.

5

What happened after that? The minutes and hours after Ben's email?

Food probably. Coffee, shit, and then food; that was usually how it went.

But there was something on the edge of it, the growing understanding that the dream and Ben's email were related.

Maybe I should beg off, tell him I have developed an allergy to water or got A.I.D.S. or something.

"AIDS? Really?" Muttered that as I rummaged in the back of my truck.

A nearby crow cawed in agreement.

Was the crow talking to me? I think it was looking right at me.

There was a feeling in the air, alien, like being on another planet or *something* now that I am going deeper into my recollections---

Things my senses filed away even if I wasn't picking up on them at the time.

"David Myer," straightforward and then almost sing-song. "David Myer."

The cop. Almost forgot that. He was waiting for me out by the truck.

No, not a cop; Homeland Security. Dressed like the Mormons do
when going door to door. He was fanning himself with my
passport, smiling but not smiling.

"You're a long way from home," he says, easy going but not.

"I'm travelling." Struggling to keep up a harmless smile and polite
tone of voice. Were my eyes hard and angry? Probably.
So were his.

"System says it's been three weeks since your last work
assignment."

I stood there, composing myself, willing my anger back down.

"Is that a problem? If you checked my account you can see I have
money, haven't been panhandling---"

My passport is held very loosely in his fingers. Will he drop it?
Laugh as I pick it up? Kick me as I'm bent over? There are cameras
around but Homeland Security can hack into those.

"Where have you been staying?" He asks, pinching the corner of my
passport. "System doesn't show any signs of lodging."

Busted. His smile tells me that. He glances over at my truck and
then winks at me. What can I say?

"Look, I may be Homeland Security but this is my town and we
don't like drifters. I'm sure you're a *nice guy* but maybe this town
has gotten a little boring for you."

There's nothing to do but smile and nod and agree. I reached for
my passport expecting him to pull it away with a cruel laugh. He let
me grab it and nodded again.

"I'm sure I'll see you again, David Myer."

6

"He was saying your name like that, just like this ghost or whatever the fuck it is?" Marcus asks.

"Yeah, I forgot about that."

"What about the rest of your day?" Ben, leaning forward.

"We've been waiting so long!" The Invisible Man, it was the first time he had said anything more than my name.

All my friends looked at me.

"You need to keep going," Ben, even he looked rattled.

"I got in my truck and drove to the next town."

7

Looking back I kept turning the dream over and over in my head:
Was it a good or a bad omen? Would one of my friends turn me
onto a new job or would one of us drown? Would the beauty of the
wild river finally clear my head or would I fight with one or more of
the people I am closest to and lose them for good?
Unknown.
At some point that same day of the dream I emailed Ben back.
Tried to be casual, like to think I was, but maybe my response was
like the smiles I gave the barista; easily seen through.
Should have I bowed out of the trip rather than risk something bad
happening?
Now: Yes. I should have seen the warning in the dream.
Then: *You are being ridiculous. Besides, everything is in motion.*
Everything is in motion. When you repeat that expression like a
mantra it tends to get more ominous, adds a shiver to your skin,
gets you looking over your shoulder.

The dream has always been a warning, a red light on the dashboard:
Stop. Look around. Think---something is not right.
Whether leading to something good or something bad, it's a bright
red light demanding awareness and alertness.

It could be that something big is about to happen or it could be that something is going on with me that I have been ignoring; it could be an illness or it could be my frame of mind. Looking back, Ben's email probably triggered it. I was happy to see his address in my inbox. I had said things to him that I regretted---said things to *all of them* that I regretted. That had led to days of radio silence. And then the days became weeks.

Initial thoughts: *Fuck them. I mean, if they really are my best friends they would have been more understanding, especially after what I went through.*

Thoughts after cooling down: *I don't want to lose my friends. Also, I have to admit I really fucked up.*

The gist of Ben's message was that the three of them had been planning a raft trip and wanted me to come along. I know them, knew it wasn't that simple; the three of them had probably been trading emails and texts and phone calls: *Should we ask David? Does he even want to hang out with us anymore? Do we want* him *hanging out with* us? *I mean, after what happened.*

Guilty.

In my defense they hadn't been supportive during the situation that caused the rift. I hate that shit; people getting all judgey---not just letting what I lost and my guilt be punishment enough.

Another reason the email was not responded to immediately was money. My friends had grown up careers and disposable income; not me. The email just sitting there made me anxious; the more time I went without replying the odds increased that one of them would take it as a snub. Not Ben, he was too laid back, but one of the other two would get judgey. They had probably already texted Ben: *Has he responded to the email? No? Guess he still wants to be a dick.*

In the end I decided to fuck my already fucked up finanial situation even more. My response to Ben was that the trip sounded awesome---

Awesome, just using that word took me back to when we all met back in high school. That felt good. It felt weird, but it also felt good.

8

The name of the barista was Maya.

I wonder what Maya and her pale blue eyes are doing right now?

9

Since when do people feel pain in dreams?

Angela, doubt all over her face. Why would I have lied? Things were like that near the end. No, maybe they were like that the entire time but there was enough love between us to push it back into the shadows.

A dream about me telling my ex about a dream.

A group of people were near the camper, laughing. Kids. Hopefully not kids out for a bit of vandalism.

Sitting up in bed, affirming the keys were at hand in case I needed to wriggle into the driver's seat and leave my spot.

The sound of the kids dissipated. Where were they headed to? To a car that would take them to the town I had left? Maybe one of them was seeing Maya; maybe one of them was fucking her---I could see it, them kissing, her stroking his big dick before---

Angela got back in my head, how she always doubted me.

Why would I have lied about feeling pain in dreams?

She could be such a *shit* sometimes---

No, this is not the place for negative thoughts. This may be my last chance to send love out to the people in my past. Not being entirely altruistic; I've always understood that different sorts of energy draw like energy.

I have deep love for you, Angela, I always will. Wherever you are, I hope you're happy.

Maya, too. Hope she has a good life with a minimum of older men gawking at her as I did.

The dream and the kids, that was the day I got the email. Secondary and then local highways took me from the greens of the valley over the mountains and across rolling scrubland. Each town I came across seemed smaller than the one that had preceded it. When night came the truck was pulled down a side road that I had taken before; a hidden place to camp on what had been BLM land. Had it become private property? All I knew was that it was dark and it was a good time to stop driving. The only sounds out there were the insects and the wind rolling through the openness. The moon came out to light the contours of the surrounding ridges. I climbed into the back and drank from my flask. Fewer and fewer cars came down the main road as the night deepened. Eventually I slept.

10

"It's only been eleven months." Lee, softly. When she got quiet it was worse somehow.

There was nothing I could say in response. Leaning forward, grabbing another beer, watching the walls of the canyon retreat as we entered another wide valley.

"And...you're scamming on girls young enough to be your kid," she continued with a bitter smile.

You think I did that on purpose, don't you? Fuck you. Go fuck yourself.

I did not say that; I knew her, could see she was on the verge of exploding.

"Lee...I was there," Marcus says. "I saw how much of a mess David was, give him a break."

She just faces forward and shakes her head before tossing a can into the stream. None of us dared to mention it.

"David Myer!" The voice seemed to be coming from a grove of trees off to our right.

"Now he's in the woods," Ben says mildly.

"What do you say, David? Want to go in the woods and look for mushrooms?" Lee, you can almost taste the acid in her voice.

Marcus winces. I struggle with my emotions.

Fuck you, Lee. Seriously---get fucked.

"Keep going," Ben, gently. He is too far to touch my shoulder but does it with his voice.

"Why? This situation is tied into the dream, or at least that's what you guys think."

Silence. Was that a bird or a man whistling in the woods?

"Just get us the fuck out of here with the story." Marcus, his voice a sigh.

11

My alarm woke me at 5:40---

That is a safe assumption because I always set my alarm so I could catch the sunrises in the desert. I had become so OCD about it that I would look up when the sun would rise on my phone.

I can see myself, sitting on the hood of my truck and hugging myself not because I felt cold...

It was happiness, something that took a couple of minutes to recognize; that strange but welcome feeling of contentment.

Graffiti I had forgotten about on a wall I passed everyday.

Everything felt calm out there, wild but calm. The light put on an amazing show before the pinks and oranges dissipated. The show ended meaning it was time to find coffee and meet up with the others.

The first town I came across was little more than a general store and a scattering of ramshackle looking farm houses and mobile homes. An older man ran the store. He had glasses that made his eyes look huge and dark blue suspenders. The old man was smiling but it was a wary smile; maybe I looked like a drifter or maybe they just didn't get many strangers out there.

"Do you have coffee?" I asked.

Another local called out. The old man looked over to acknowledge the other fellow. As they talked I wondered if I was being blown off, finally the old man looked back at me.

"Yep. You got a travel cup or do you need one of mine?"

"I'll take one of yours if you can spare it."

He nodded and walked over to a large thermos behind him. It was clear there would be no chat, no inquiries about where I was headed; so much for friendly country folk. The styrofoam cup was set on the counter and the price given.

"Hey, my friends and I are going down the river," I said. "You got any advice?"

He got a strange look on his face. It reminded me of Angela's expression when she was removing the black thread in the dream.

"Don't do it," he replied.

Before I could ask for clarification a group of locals came through the front door. All of them looked at me as if I were a zoo exhibition. It was time to go.

12

The final road to the river was undivided asphalt that gave way to rough gravel after a couple of miles. I bounced along in an aura of dust, thinking about the dream.

Since when do people feel pain in dreams?

And the shop owner: *Don't do it.*

I found a lot guarded by a dusty porto-potti. There was a trail that seemed to go in the direction of the river so I followed it until I was sitting on the bank sipping burnt coffee and feeling the texture of the styrofoam on my lips.

Don't do it.

Had his voice become gruffer on those three words? And what was with that *nod*? He had definitely nodded.

Okay, you are being ridiculous. He and his bumpkin buddies probably have a lot of secret fishing spots they don't want us tourists finding, that's all.

That was a good point. Unfortunately it didn't quell my feelings of uneasiness. The water moved slowly but looked clear. I lowered myself onto what little shore the river offered, a bit of sand a foot or so square. The water was surprisingly cold for that late in the year---

I was being watched. An animal? Some deer across the river.

Across the stream was a bluff that looked a few feet high and behind it some raspy looking trees. I couldn't see any animals... And then the shadows changed, something was definitely moving; it looked man shaped. Someone stepping from behind a tree and walking off deeper into the woods across the river.

13

"You saw something and you didn't warn us." Lee, reaching for a bottle of whisky. Not a question, a statement. No, an *accusation*.

"Would you have given up this trip if I had told you any of this?" I asked, biting back my resentment but still spitting some out.

"Okay, you two, chill out." Ben, holding his hands up. "To be fair, David, every time you've had the dream something major has happened."

"Normal shit, not the Invisible Man or anything else," I replied. The light was changing, creating more shadows. It wasn't just the sun moving behind clouds or over mountains it was something else; you could feel it.

14

I walked back to the parking lot. My feet were colder than the rest of my body and every bit of dirt that got on my shoes stuck to them. A lifted Ford pickup had parked next to my car. It looked too new to belong to a local, had to be one of my friends. The side windows were tinted too deeply to see inside but I guessed it belonged to Lee. Hearing muted country music I understood that I had guessed correctly. The music stopped and the driver's side door opened to a fanfare of chimes. Lee walked around the back of the truck and nodded when she saw me. I nodded back; that's how things have been with us since we were teenagers.

"I thought you had a Benz," she said.

"The transmission went out, couldn't afford to get it fixed."

She just looked at me, I could see the awkwardness I felt reflected in her posture. Lee looked around, sipped from the bottle of beer I hadn't noticed in her hand.

"We are really out here, aren't we?" I offered.

"Looks that way."

Why had she been the first one? Now we were obligated to hammer words together to piece together some sort of a conversation. I say *hammer* because it was always work, the two of us being friends. Lee looked even bulkier. Not fat, though at our ages we were all thickening, more muscular. She had always been solid, even back in high school.

"You check out the river?" She asked with the bottle up to her lips.

"Yeah. Water is surprisingly cold."

Lee grunted and nodded, taking her beer and walking to the other end of the parking lot. Our conversation was over.

A newer Suburban pulled in the lot as I took my last sip of coffee. Two men were inside, one black and one Asian. Lee raised her beer at them. The driver honked in return. The truck parked, the doors opened, and the two men climbed out to walk towards me. They were smiling but there was some guardedness to it; I wanted to say there was some shame, as well, but that was probably what I wanted to see. I pulled each one into a hug in turn. Lee walked over and shook their hands. All four of us stood in silence for a few moments, Lee was the first to break it.

"This place will probably fill up by mid afternoon."

"I don't know what you were thinking, B," Marcus winced.

"What?" Ben seemed dazed, had probably already smoked.

"We're in hillbilly central," Lee nodded. "They'll be out here tonight, mobs of them listening to bro country and drinking Coors Light and looking for city folk to harass."

What was she worried about? Lee has the biggest arms of all of us with a scowl and flattop to match.

"I hadn't thought about that," Ben, looking mildly concerned.

"Come on, you guys are being ridiculous," I said.

"Says the only white male here." Ben, frowning.

All three of them looked over at me. I couldn't tell if they were fucking with me or not.

And then a phantom tugs at my scalp; the dream.

"It's going to be fine." I say this firmly and then smile. Hopefully it looks natural.

"This is going to be the best thirtieth reunion of all," Ben says.

"What?" I ask.

Ben and Marcus looked at each other.

"Yeah...I thought this could be our thirtieth anniversary celebration."

"Why not."

If this were a movie, good time rock music would be cued, the rest of us would open beers of our own, and there would be a montage of us laughing and generally having a good time.

This is not a movie, this really happened...

No, this is still happening.

15

"You know why we're not buddies." Lee shot me a look. She was trying to look hard but there were cracks with softness oozing out. Yeah, I know. I *knew*.

"It's starting to get dark," Ben observes.

"It's fucking two in the afternoon," Lee snarls. "This is...I don't know what the fuck this is."

"Keep going, David," Ben adds.

16

Ravens were croaking in the trees and circling as we set up our tent fifty yards from the river.

"I think we should load the raft and put it in the river tonight."

Marcus. Ben may have suggested the trip but Marcus was taking charge.

"You're not worried about people taking shit out of it?" I asked.

"This isn't the city. Besides, we'll be literally a hundred feet away." He replied.

"Literally?"

"Okay, maybe not *literally* a hundred feet but we'll hear people coming through camp."

But what if they drifted alongside in a raft and silently took our supplies.

That thought, unvoiced.

Feeling eyes in the closest tree I looked up. A raven was staring at me, a big one. It croaked twice, bobbed its head, and flew off.

I am obsessing over the memory, convincing myself the bird said "David Myer."

Most of the ease we had felt in the past had come back but there was still a sense of guardedness; I felt it, I was picking it up from

Marcus and Ben. Lee? We had never been that close, friends only because both of us hung out with Marcus and Ben...and Angela. Thinking of my wife, emotions returned. I walked off after telling the others I was headed for the bathroom. Walking back I saw the three of them in a close circle, talking and smiling, even Lee was smiling. They didn't register my presence until I was close enough to smell Marcus' cologne; cologne, on a camping trip. Only Marcus.

"This place is really remote," Lee said. "I'm glad I've got good clearance."

"Yeah, only locals come out here, it's easy to get lost."

Locals. That word had become ominous. All of us looked at each other.

"Come on, this is going to be an awesome trip." Ben--should he have been vaping out there? Wasn't weed illegal in a national forest?

And there were a *lot* of ravens---would they shit on our tent?

A truck was pulling in. Truck.

Here come the locals, the hillbillies with their bro country and shotgun racks. "Y'all smell like city folk, with your shoes and mouth fulla teeth."
The truck had a bunch of camping gear in the back and circled the roads looking for their site. I saw a Black Lives Matter sticker on the back bumper next to one proclaiming Bernie 2020. City Folk.

"Looks like hipsters." Lee, opening another beer.

Their site was next to ours. A few minutes later two Subarus and a Prius rolled in and parked at adjacent sites.

"Looks like we got lucky, guys." Ben, his voice raspy from vaping.

"As long as they don't play any reggae." Marcus opened one of Lee's beers. "I fucking hate reggae."

All of us did. The four of us had a collection of random dislikes and likes that all lined up. If you spent a few minutes with us you'd wonder what we had in common; that took hours or even days to be revealed.

17

"Da-vid M-y-er!"

The Invisible Man was back. Nearly singing my name, throwing out his tune and then laughing happily. Who the fuck was he? *Where* was he? I wanted to see him but feared when we did it would be horrific---

What was he?

Marcus asked for the whisky bottle. Lee tossed it at him: Cork popped. Long Drink.

"I was looking through our yearbook right before I left..."

Thanks, Marcus, thanks for throwing kerosene on Lee's resentment fire.

"What went wrong?"

He asked that after turning to me plaintively with a little bit of accusation blended in for flavor.

What went wrong? I had no idea she was allergic to fucking mushrooms.

Lee had her back to us but I could feel the anger coming off in waves. She was probably grinding her teeth like she always did when pissed off.

"Did you have the wrong mushroom?" Marcus, uncorking the bottle again.

"No, it was an amanita muscaria," I said numbly. "I triple checked, followed all the instructions---"

"I don't want to fucking hear about this!" Lee snarled.

Our world grew silent aside from the natural sounds: Water against the raft. A bird off in the woods---

"Da-v-id M-yer!"

And that fucker, of course.

No one had to prompt me to continue that time.

18

The Lead Hipster approached our campground. He had a smile
semi-hidden in his bushy brown beard. Lead Hipster made a
beeline for Marcus and extended his hand.

"I thought it would be all hillbillies out here. I'm Jason."

We introduced ourselves. Jason gestured at the dozen or so people
climbing out of the cars and setting up their camps.

"I just wanted to introduce myself. We're gonna have some fun but
if it gets to be too much please come over and let us know. We don't
want to be *those people*."

He was still smiling but something had changed with his face;
maybe he had picked up on Marcus' cologne.

"Thanks."

He walked off. The four of us looked at each other.

"Seemed like a nice guy."

"Yeah, I think our rafting trip is off to a good start."

I smiled and clinked bottles with the three of them but inside---
Inside I kept replaying the dream and seeing the old guy in the
store and whatever had been watching me from across the water.

Lee and Marcus struggled to get the raft down to the river. I carried
the pump and Ben was in charge of filling the valves with air.

"How is such a pothead so mechanically competent?"

"I've explained this before, dude--" Ben, immediately losing his train of thought. Marcus caught onto that and laughed, even Lee smiled.

I was standing off to the side, outside the circle just a little but even if it was just a little I could still feel it: A cold spot. Dead air. Marcus looked over at me and smiled. It was an old smile, from before all the angry emails back and forth. He backed up a step and nodded at me. It felt good.

"You still doing good?"

"Yeah, full recovery. Ready to row."

I made a muscle, Ben looked over.

"That's pathetic, dude."

"Well, Lee has muscles for all four of us."

She looked over at me not smiling, no different from how it had ever been.

The raft was filling quickly. The only sounds out there was the moving water, the air passing from the pump through the valves, and insects singing in the grass. When the chambers were full the four of us lifted the raft into the water. It was huge, looked as big as my truck. Ben saw us appraising it and gave his raft the thumbs up.

"Go big or go home, right?"

Laughter. Everything felt good in that moment, light and easy and carefree.

That moment would pass.

19

"We're not safe because of you."

Should I respond to her or ignore it?

"You mean because I didn't tell you guys about the dream?"

Lee pulled her oar out of the water and set it across her lap. Her voice was steady but her back was still to me and I could feel her anger.

"We're only safe when it's all five of us," she said.

"Come on, Lee—" I replied defensively.

"She's right." Marcus, looking into the woods where the Invisible Man had seemingly been calling from.

"Do you really believe we would have been protected as long as it was *all five of us*?"

My tone was sarcastic but inside there was anxiety: *He's right. It has felt different since we all met up.*

"The last time I had the dream I got $25k out of the blue," Ben said.

"The time before that I broke a molar on some sushi."

He frowned and picked up his bottle of beer before continuing.

"I have no idea how you break a tooth on fish but I did."

'I'm fucking sorry, okay!" Now I was the angry one shouting.

Even Lee looked taken aback; I am normally not a shouter.

"Angela never told me she was allergic to mushrooms," I continued, my voice still raised. "In fact, we had taken psychedelic mushrooms before. So---"

Rage. Sadness. Guilt. Words gone.

I let it go, just screamed as loud and as raw as I could. It sounded like a dying animal and then there was this charged silence. For a few moments.

"Da-vid M-y-er!"

20

I need to be away from here, from where I am at this moment, from all the bullshit with the four of us on that stupid raft.
I am going back to the last minutes everything was sane, the last time the sun set and life felt normal and safe.

We walked back to our campsite. More beer, memories coming back, good ones, easy laughter and yet---
It wasn't the same. There was a wall between my friends and I, not so tall I couldn't see them, but there was a wall. And I had put it up. Not on purpose; not that such a detail made things any easier.

The sun went over the mountains. Despite it being mid-year a chill found us. I started a fire. Ben had brought some meat and began seasoning it for a group bar-be-que. The four of us drank more beer and ate the charred yet raw meat. The juice running down my chin reminded me of the dream, drops of blood down black string. The hipsters were listening to the Decemberists and some other Portland music. Time passed, more memories and laughter drifted over the flames. A headlamp came bobbing towards us, closing the distance between the music and our voices. Jacob. We had some meat left and offered it. He begged off with a laugh, saying he was already full.

"Hey...you guys seem cool---"

Was that what he said? It was something like that but the exact words...

Lost. This is where memories still to break apart or maybe melt. You'll understand soon enough.

Jacob pulled a pipe out of a jacket pocket. It looked like ivory but I doubt it was: An old sailor's head, watch cap, scowl, and chin beard. A clear image surrounded by ones out of focus.

Weed. He's smoking us out.

Why not? The four of us exchanged looks, even Marcus shrugged and smoked.

After passing it in a circle a few times whatever was in the bowl was done. We chatted with Jacob a bit more and then he had to get back to his own people. Ben watched him go and then spoke to us in a low voice:

"That wasn't just weed."

"What?" Marcus, concerned. No, Marcus looked *anxious*.

"Just enjoy the ride," Ben shrugged. "Everything is in motion."

"He dosed us? I'm fucking kicking that hipster's ass!" Lee said.

"You're not kicking anyone's ass," Marcus, firmly. Knowing he was the only one who could talk sense to Lee.

She stared into flames as if meaning to use her anger to make them rise.

"He dosed us; that is not cool," she added, a little more resigned.

"No, he offered us a pipe and we willingly smoked it. You assumed it was just weed; you have to live with the danger of just assuming things."

Ben looked happy, probably looking forward to whatever trip we were about to go on.

"When a dude in the woods offers you a pipe that looks like a sailor's head," he nodded. "You have to know that you're going to get fucked up."

21

"I am going to put out there again the possibility that this is not happening."

After saying that Ben looked over the side of the raft. How deep was it? How far down could he see? I wondered that for reasons I am not comfortable with going into yet.

"Fuck you, Ben," Lee growled. "I feel my sunburn, you can't feel pain in dreams."

The rest of us looked at each other and she caught on.

"Aside from that dream," Lee conceded.

"You can feel pain when tripping, I will attest to that."

None of us had a response to Ben's observation.

"That night we smoked with the hipsters---who has any memory of that."

I did so I shared the admittedly faulty memories I started sharing with you.

22

There were whoops and cheers coming from the other campsites. The pre-recorded music stopped. People were drumming and chanting.

"Fucking hipsters," Lee muttered before standing up with a jerk.

"Did anyone else see that?"

"What?" Marcus, standing up himself.

"I thought it was a man...but then it was a deer or half deer half man---"

"A centaur," Ben nodded. "Awesome."

I didn't look; the last thing I needed to see was a fucking centaur. The woods were coming to life around us. No, *life* wasn't the right word.

"They came through here." My voice was a whisper but my friends looked over.

"Who?" Lee. I remember how high she looked at that point.

"The pioneers...some died out here."

It was in my head, starting to haunt me, I didn't want to be alone with the ghosts.

"Ah, come on, man...not that shit, not out here." Marcus---was he angry with me?

"This is you, this is your shit," Lee. No doubt she was angry with me. "It's like what happened several months ago---"

Yes, I am remembering it. She was talking about *breaking the circle* that night.

"No, it was like when he got better." Ben, his words sounded thick. Like syrup.

"Are we doing this now?" Marcus, hugging himself.

Are we doing this now?

I remember that. That conversation happened...I'm pretty sure.

After that I have a memory of Jacob coming over. He was nude. There was something on his skin that looked like blood when he stood close to the fire.

Relax. It's not blood, you're just high.

No, it looked like blood, drying blood, it did---

What part of "you're fucking high" didn't you get?

And then we were in their campground. All of them were naked, some were smeared with whatever was on Jacob. Marcus asked what it was.

Some short beardo with a large penis shook his head.

"Not yet, man---you want to smoke some more?"

Marcus took the sailor pipe, took a greedy hit.

Marcus: Mr. Khakis and Enjoys Doing Taxes.

"Dude...you got a big cock." Lee, to the beardo.

Beardo didn't seem to hear her, he passed the pipe to Ben and then went off to dance to the drums. Lee followed him, I'm nearly certain of that.

Memories drag other memories into the light and so on:
I remember people dancing out of the light and when they came back they were freshly smeared with what the fire made look like blood. Marcus and I looked at each other and followed them into the darkness. Neither of us had a light with us.
"Shit."
"What?"
"I bumped into something."
He was leaning down, feeling for whatever he had walked into.
"It feels like a table, a wood table---*fuck!*"
"What?"
"A body." He sounded scared.
"A *body*?"
"I think it's the centaur."
That made me curious but not curious enough to touch it.

We found our way back to the fire. There was more dancing. On the edge of the light there were mats....people were laughing, some were fucking...fucking like animals. And laughing. A woman sat next to me, leaned into me. Took my hand. I see Angela in the memory but I know that is just my mind playing tricks on me---

It felt good to be close to someone again, feel their warm, feel them squeezing my hand. She began petting my hair. A weird look took over her face.

"It feels weird, like there's a scar up there..."

23

"You did not just tell me that I cheated on Phillip. Fuck."

Lee was doubled over, both hands on her hand.

"I don't....*know*?" Marcus, looking to me for help.

"Sorry, dude, I'm pretty sure you did." Yeah, that was petty of me but she had been a non-stop asshole.

"No one's memories are solid. It may be a false memory."

Why Ben felt the need to sooth Lee I have no idea.

24

The next a hundred percent clear memory:

Light coming through fabric. I was in the tent alone. No hangover,

in fact I felt good. After all that partying it had to be late, right?

No, it was a little after seven. How much sleep had I had?

The other three were sitting around the dead fire. It looked like

they had been up awhile. Wait---

What had happened to all the hipster tents? Had they come down

during all the wildness?

Their cars were gone, too.

"They're gone." Lee. Had I really seen her giving the Beardo a

handjob?

Not just a handjob...

"How?"

"I guess they wanted to get an early start."

"I don't know how."

I agreed with Marcus; my last memory was things still going

strong---

It had to be well past midnight at that point, right?

Was it seven the *following* morning? Had we slept more than

twenty-four hours?

No, it was the *next* morning.

"Break down the tent, dude. The river waits."

Ben. He had something smeared on his face--

The centaur blood. No, it was a deer; a sacrifice.

I got up and looked at him closer. It was strawberry jelly.

Maybe I had imagined everything.

"Was any of that real?" I asked myself but aloud.

Marcus looked over at me. He looked tired, maybe smoking more had done it.

"Let's not get into that now."

We packed up the tent and then lugged our supplies to the raft. When the others were out of sight I made a detour through the hipster camp. Everything looked normal, no disturbed earth from the wild dancing I had thought I saw. No splatters or pools of dried blood.

But that really happened, I'm sure of it...pretty sure.

No, you were just high as fuck. Let it go. Really, just let it go.

It was bugging me, though, it still does.

25

"It's a hundred miles. Should take two days, maybe three depending on how often we stop."

"Is the current that fast?"

"In places like this. In some it's still."

I wanted to bring up the previous night but the others didn't seem to want to talk about it. Why didn't they want to talk about it? Pressing the issue felt wrong, like I'd be pushing my luck when things were still delicate between my friends and I. Lee and I pushed off.

"Shit, it gets deep fast. Hold my beer." Lee, struggling to heave herself over the side. She was in a front corner along with Marcus. Ben and I took the back. All of us were sloppy with the oars, some were too casual, Lee too forceful; it took awhile for us to get in sync. It was beautiful out there. After a while we rowed less, began letting the river control the raft, just drifting until we got too close to the shore.

"I can see why you want to leave the world behind." Ben, smiling at me.

It looked genuine; the way things had been that felt good.

"I don't want to leave the world behind, I just don't want to waste my time on stupid shit."

"Like the stupid shit you did with Angela?" Lee, of course.

So...we were going *there*?

"Angela should be out here, enjoying this with us."

She added that before shaking her head and opening another beer.

There was nothing I could say. Yeah, there had been five of us and now there were four of us because of me. Marcus looked back at me. I could see by his face he still cared for me but the whole Angela thing---

He couldn't let it go either.

I had to look away from them, at a couple of ravens in a tree. They seemed to be watching us pass by.

26

"Da-vid My-er! Oh, *Da-v-id!*"

"Maybe it's the man from the house."

"Fuck, Lee, we're not bringing that shit up; not out here!"

Wow, Ben was raising his voice. That was only the second or third time I had heard him raise his voice.

"We only stopped him when there were *five* of us."

Lee said that and then gave me a dirty look. It wasn't the time or the place to bring up the fucking *man from the house* but she just had to be selfish I guess.

Don't be a chickenshit, look in the windows, you know they're in there.
Five teenagers staring at an old house, egging each other on.
Angela and I had been holding hands, Lee had been pretending not to see that but you feel her anger.
All of us had felt weird shit from the house. There were stories around the neighborhood about Satanists that had lived there or something...
Yeah, not going back to that memory---not out here.

27

A better recollection, our first hours on the river:

The mood was sour for a while but the scenic beauty beguiled us.

"I didn't know this river went through lava flows."

"Yeah, damn, check out those rocks..."

"Wow...this is awesome."

The current slowed to a crawl. It must have been past noon because we were hungry. We took cold cuts from the icebox and made sandwiches. Marcus ate as if he had been ravenous, it reminded me of the night before; wildness.

The river narrowed. We were in the woods again, trees forming a canopy over the slow moving water. There was something coppery in the air---blood? Had a deer been taken down by a mountain lion nearby or something? I wasn't the only one who smelled it, Marcus looked concerned as well.

"Did something get---"

"Shhh!" Lee, staring into the trees off to our left.

She cowed us into silence. With the current stilled it was incredibly quiet, no birds or insects or anything except---

Something rustling off in the trees where Lee was staring. It was a man...but something was *off* about him: His clothes looked weird, old fashioned. He was scowling at us and had a dark chin beard. Was it really dark or was it just that the man was pale? How was he so pale out there in the desert?

"Let's get out of here," Marcus, starting to row.

And then Lee looked scared. No, she looked terrified. *Lee.*

"Row, *fucking row!*" She yelled.

I didn't see what she saw but the desperation in her voice got me rowing like I had yet to row on that trip. Even Ben started putting his back into it. After a minute or two all of us were gasping for breath. The river widened and the canopy of trees had fallen away, growing sparser in the distance. We stopped rowing. All of us were winded enough that it took a while to speak.

"What did you see?" Marcus asked.

"I don't want to fucking talk about it." Lee. Was she shaking?

Lee set down her oar and began rummaging in a duffle right behind her. She pulled out a bottle of whiskey and took a long drink before offering it to Marcus who shook his head. I took a sip as did Ben.

"Homespun," he said, tossing the bottle back up front. "That was the word I was looking for."

"What?"

"Back in the old days, like pioneer times; they called the clothes they made themselves *homespun.*"

The pioneer times. Good, I wasn't the only one who had seen that or gotten that feeling from the man on the bank.

Lee was staring into the river not unlike how she had stared into the fire the night before. It was as if she were trying to force what she had seen into the darkness.

"His boots were not touching the ground," she said hoarsely.

"What?" Marcus, laughing. It was uncomfortable laughter. Nervous laughter.

"It was a shadow. It was all the shadows in the woods making it looking that way."

Ben said that but it was clear he didn't believe that. Not at all.

28

"Flashbacks, that's what they called them." Marcus---was he talking to himself?

"Flashbacks?" I asked.

"People feeling the effects of acid long after they took it," Ben nodded as he took a long hit off his vape pen. "You think we saw that pioneer dude floating because of what we smoked last night?"

"Yeah." No, Marcus didn't know *what* he was thinking—his frown said that; he was desperate to come up with *any* explanation.

The current had picked up some. We all had to be vigilant on the oars or risk being pushed towards shore---

Where the ghosts of pioneers await...

Not helping. Not at all.

"We didn't see shit." Lee. Flatly. Taking a long drink off her beer. The conversation died. The only sounds were nature: Water lapping against the hull. Slight wind in the surrounding trees. The croak of a raven. Laughter.

Come on...maybe we are still high. I didn't hear that.

Looking around at the faces of my friends I understood that I probably had.

"We're freaking out," Ben, deciding to attempt and dissipate the anxiety on the raft. "We're seeing shit...it's that stuff we smoked, that's all, our brains are still picking up on things that aren't there..."

"Or maybe smoking it opened us to see things we don't normally see," Lee, the last of us I'd expect to say such a thing.

"We need to stop." Marcus, firmly but with his voice going up half an octave:

I need you guys to stop. Talking about this is freaking me out.

"I'm sorry. I fucked things up and I understand things will never be the same."

No one responded though I could see the three of them thinking. Were they waiting for something else? An explanation? I had given them one at the time but it had never been accepted or understood.

"You made a mistake---"

"You fucked up and it got one of us killed." Lee, of course.

"If this has pissed you guys off so much, why did you ask---"

"Shhh!" Lee again; this *shhing* was becoming a thing with her.

She was probably honing in on the laughter: Childish laughter, the laughter of playing children.

"We need to keep rowing---"

"No, I want to see who it is."

Why? Could the sound lead us to anything good?

The sound was coming from the woods off to our left.

"I saw some kids, girls I think."

"Yeah, they're wearing dresses."

"Old shit," Ben softly. "We need to keep rowing."

"White dresses."

"We need to keep rowing." Ben, more firmly.

We picked up our oars and fell back into rhythm.

29

"Da-vid My-e-r, we're waitin' for ya!"

Did the Invisible Man look like Mr. Chin Beard from the first day?

"It was Angela who knew the spell." Ben had his eyes closed, and was leaving the rowing to the rest of us.

Don't be a chickenshit, look in the windows, you know they're in there.

So, all of us had looked in the windows of that house.

We looked in the windows and then we went to Lee's to drink beer in the garage.

The man in the house had followed us.

All of us saw him out of the corner of our eyes---

Bad shit began happening to all five of it, too much to count as shitty luck.

We all started having the dream---yes, that is when it happened. I forgot but, yes, and it was all five of us.

Then Angela found a spell. Every cliche from movies you can imagine: Candles, chanting, holding hands with our eyes closed.

The dreams continued but the bad luck ended.

And the man from the house was out of our life---

"Da-vid M-yer! Finally found ya!"

---for a while...

30

"What is your pain level?"

"Pardon?" My pain was bad, making words was too much work.

"On a scale of one to ten." The doctor needed a breath mint. It smelled like he had a bad tooth.

"Twelve point three," I said weakly.

He chuckled at that, more bad breath.

"Your organs are having a bad day---"

"Is that how my wife died?"

That caught the doctor off guard, I could see it.

He was looking down at my hand---was he thinking of taking it? The doctor looked up at me, pulling his Calm Professional mask back on.

"I don't know, David. I know this is hard but you have to focus on *you* right now."

"She saved us," Rambling. They had me on pain drugs---Oxy? Whatever it was made me babble and yet failed to kill the pain.

"We need to---"

"I know, *focus on me*; my organs are having a bad day. I didn't know doctors said things like that..."

My babble was throwing him off. If I didn't work with my doctor I could die; that was clear through the pain and the drugs.

"Sorry," I said. "What do we need to do?"

"We have a new drug regimen. It has proven successful in a few subjects but you would need to sign consent forms."

"Okay...you look worried..."

"I'm not worried, but there are side effects."

"Like what?"

He was struggling to put them in terms that would sound Calm and Professional, that was easy to see.

"Have you ever done psychedelic drugs?" He asked, clearly uncomfortable with the question.

"Have you?"

Dr. Halitosis blushed. Blushed. I really needed to get a new medical plan.

"No, but I am familiar with the effects."

"Yes, I have," I finally answered his question.

"So you know how they distort reality?."

"Yes. That is what this drug regimen will do?"

"It could, yes."

"Well...it would be better than dying so bring me the forms and a pen."

"There's a bit more to the process than that but, okay, I'm glad you're open to trying something new. We want you to live."

Something about those five words and the painfully earnest expression on his face---

The doctor cared about me...something about that just threw open the door to a whole bunch of shit percolating inside me.

"She saved us."

Those words and then I just burst, doubling over and sobbing.

The doctor stared at me for a few moments and then left the room.

31

The first afternoon on the river passed like this:

Beer. Lots of drifting. A little rowing. Not talking about how I had fucked things up or whomever was laughing on shore. The laughter sound you could write off as the wind through the trees or a bird---it wasn't like a name was distinctly being called out. Lighthearted nostalgia; one of us, uncomfortable with the tension, would recall a story from our collective past and the others would chime in and eventually we would get lost in the past and laugh and feel good but...

There was an edge to everything, *shadows*.

"We need to start looking for a place to camp," Lee said.

"Oh man, I am not looking forward to this; four people in their late forties who have been drinking beer all day---"

"The farts!" Marcus interjected.

We all laughed, even Lee chuckled a little. She looked at me and nodded, for once it wasn't hostile. *Had* I seen her fucking that beardo with the big dick? Riding him, grinding him into the ground?

Pretty sure, not a hundred percent, maybe ninety.

Had I been jealous?

As if you ever had a right to that.

We would have made quite the couple, the butch chick and the skinny Goth dude. But...I was into Angela. And, once I found out she was into me that was it. Somehow all of us stayed friends but Lee had cooled on me.

"That looks like a good place."

"I don't know." *Because it's on the same side of the river as the laughter.*

"Come on, it looks decent. Besides, the light is dying."

Did we really want to use the word *dying* out there?

We rowed towards the place Marcus had pointed out, Lee leaping out as the raft ran aground. She was surprisingly graceful. I watched as she pulled the bow rope, her nipples hard through her shirt. I found myself getting aroused, going back to the memory of her coming as she rode the beardo's big cock---

"No daydreaming, dude, come on."

Ben, whacking me on the shoulder. I needed to get up, help drag the raft onto the shore. Maybe no one would notice my erection. I jumped out and helped secure the raft. Marcus and Ben were talking about the campsite, where to set up our tent. Lee looked at the front of my shorts and then up at my face, her own face a blank.

32

Further down the river I leave that last bit out.

None of my friends want to hear about me noticing Lee's nips or the resulting hard on.

There was a time when she was softer; another thing I have to accept blame for.

Further down the river I *did* restate my certainty that Lee had fucked the Beardo. As I said that I was looking at Ben who shook his head.

Yeah, it was petty of me. All of Lee's hostility I earned, I get that...I should have just accepted it without serving up my own pettiness.

33

The first twilight on the river we pulled the raft onto the shore and looked for a place to set up the tent.

"I need to piss, I'll be back."

No, I needed to jerk off, to deal with my arousal so it wasn't in the way. I wasn't thinking about the scowling man or the childish laughter there was just the image of Lee's nipples through her shirt and the memory or fantasy of her fucking that guy in the dirt.

You used me.

Lee, more than thirty years younger, showing a vulnerability I hadn't known she possessed. I was young and stupid back then---*stupider.*

The arousal was gone, replaced by guilt.

I was just out there, standing in those ponderosa pines; such a beautiful place to have fucked up memories.

You ever think that all those times you wanted to leave Angela that energy may have led to what happened?

No. No means *yes* in that instance.

It's fucked up to admit but I had wishes of Angela dying. I had no violent thoughts about her, I certainly didn't hate her, but if she had succumbed to an illness or accident I would be free.

See, I was a coward like that. Still am.

I could never come out and say *I need to be alone a lot more, maybe all alone the rest of my life. I am suffocating. God, I love you, I see how good we have it, having each other, but I am miserable and I can't go on like this.*

But I didn't want to see the hurt on her face or deal with the words that would follow.

See: *Coward.*

And then I fucked up and she died.

Something was watching me. I thought it was an animal at first, maybe a mountain lion. Something wild that wanted to snack on me.

No, it was a little girl. Just a little girl in a white dress staring at me.

"Are you lost?" I asked. "Where are your mommy and daddy?"

I took a gentle step forward, crouching down to get to her level.

Ten feet away from her I picked up on her scents: Smoke. Blood. Decay.

The little girl turned and started walking off. The back of her dress was blackened and there was an arrow between her shoulder blades. I watched her walking off as I began backing away, knowing if she turned around again I would see a grinning skull.

34

I am still high. Maybe it was peyote in that pipe---can you smoke peyote?
Calm me, reasonable me, talking myself down from hysteria as I
walked back to camp. There was no way I had seen that little girl.
How was that possible?
It's possible because there was more than weed in that pipe. Fuck...that's
some crazy stuff--I wonder where we could get some more?
Lee was struggling to help Ben set up the tent. Marcus watched me
emerge from the woods.
"What did you see out there?"
I must have had a weird look on my face. Should I tell them?
Why? You'll just freak them out; how about not being a selfish bastard for
once?
"Nah, I'm just spooked from all that shit earlier."
He nodded but I could tell he wasn't satisfied.
"Let's see if we can find some deadfall for the fire."
We walked off in the direction I had gone.
"There's some, surprised I didn't see it before---"
"What did you see?" He asked firmly.
It was the last thing I wanted to talk about out there, it felt like an
invitation for everything that was watching us, just waiting for
night to fall.

"A little girl."

"A little girl?"

"Yeah. White dress. Maybe one of the kids we heard playing earlier."

Kids playing, way out in the middle of nowhere. Not impossible---Well, maybe not kids with arrows sticking out of their backs. Charred kids. Marcus looked at me. I could see him struggling to stay calm. I took his hand, he resisted a little but then relented.

"Dude...what the hell is going on out here?" He asked.

"Fuck if I know."

We gathered deadfall. Made three trips away from camp, got enough for a decent fire.

"Do we need a permit to have a fire out here?"

"Got one in my bag." Marcus, always the organized one.

Ben started the fire. Lee got a bottle of whiskey from her duffle and we passed it around. Everytime we lapsed into silence one of us would start talking, just talking about whatever: No one wanted to hear laughter or muttering or whatever the fuck we'd hear out there.

"I have a bruise on my hip."

We looked over at Marcus. It took a moment for what he said to register---

Bumping into the table, *that* had been real. If that was real then maybe the sacrificed deer/centaur was and everything else--

Or, he bumped into his truck or something.

I think all of us would have preferred that explanation.

We drained the bottle. Ben offered his vape but none of us partook. In my case I didn't want to risk altering my mind any further. When we pissed all of us---even Lee---stayed within earshot. All of us were scared even if it remained unspoken.

At that point, at least.

35

Sleep didn't come easy. I just lay there, trying to remain still and let the others sleep. Through the thin walls of the tent, I could hear the water moving and sloshing against the raft. Lee was quiet next to me. As we had drank she had been talking about her husband Paul. She talked about him how some men talk about women: Luridly. Appreciative of their bodies in detail. Lee told us about Paul's big dick and how good he was with it. Talked about it about how some guys talk about a Quarterback who throws well. Marcus, Ben, and I would exchange looks:

Great, something not to think about whenever we saw Paul again.

Paul looked like an accountant: Dorky white guy who tended to wear button down shirts and go on for hours about *Star Trek* or *Lord of the Rings*.

How was I not supposed to check out the front of his khakis if we ever hung out?

As she told us about her husband's endowment Lee was looking right at me. I looked back, thinking about the memory or fantasy of her and the beardo. And I was thinking about it lying there in the tent. Getting aroused I considered rolling on my side and taking care of it but didn't want to make a mess in my sleeping bag.

I managed to push the thoughts away but they were replaced with the scowling man on the bank. Rising, opening his arms as he drifted towards me, smiling with horrible teeth like yellow gravestones, getting closer---

A hand on my mouth: *The ghost, fuck, he got me!*

"You were whimpering," Lee whispered, her hand smelled like dirt and whiskey.

She removed the hand. I could feel her looking at me through the dark.

"I imagine we're all gonna have fucked up dreams tonight," Lee said matter of factly.

She rolled back over on her back.

When her hand had been on my face I had wanted her to come out of her sleeping bag and straddle me, ride me like she had ridden the hipster.

You used me.

And then a memory came, one of her and Angela making out; me edging closer, hoping to be included.

It was time to sleep. Or at least be silent. I rolled on my side and eventually went under.

36

In the morning we didn't want to bother with gathering wood or dealing with a fire. The four of us snacked and Marcus used the camp stove to make coffee.

"Are the ashes cool in the fire?"

Ben went over to check. He crouched down, putting his hand in the ashes. When he stiffened I thought he had burnt himself on a hot spot.

"You okay?"

Ben didn't respond, didn't move.

"Dude...did you get burned?"

Very slowly he shook his head. Ben was shaking, you could see it from a few feet away.

Ben---the laid back one, the one who never got upset.

The three of us walked over to try and determine what had rattled him. It looked like a piece of charred driftwood at first but it wasn't; it was the burnt leg bone of a child.

37

Further down the river I stop speaking. Again, I have spared them any of my lust for Lee but *did* go over how she had been going on and on about his dick.

"You guys are pussies." She smiles, it isn't a nice smile. "Are the three of you so insecure you can't hear about another guy's dick?"

"How am I supposed to hang out with him next month?"

Marcus--is he aware he's giving the oar a handjob?

Next month---he's been invited to Lee's house for something, Ben probably was as well.

You have no one to blame but yourself. Do you really think Lee would invite you after everything that happened?

No, it still stung, though.

"Hey, we haven't heard the Invisible Man in a while---"

"Da-vid M-ye-r!"

The three of us stared darkly at Ben for being a fucking idiot.

38

The second day on the raft, moving downstream, not talking.

"Maybe we should call the sheriff or the rangers."

"There's no signal out here. I recorded the GPS coordinates; we can contact the authorities when we're back in the world."

Back in the world---I wish Ben wouldn't have put it that way.

More silence. More ravens circling in the trees.

"That bone wasn't there last night; I made that fire ring from scratch."

"Do we have to talk about it?" Lee, yelling.

Marcus looked as if he had been struck.

"I'm sorry, guys, this trip has gotten a little fucked up."

There was nothing to say to that. The woods were growing sparser on either side of the river until there was nothing but scrub and rock and dirt. The valley we were passing through narrowed from miles across to hundreds of yards. The river narrowed and the current picked up speed. Our raft rocked and bobbed as the four of us struggled to keep it from dashing on the canyon walls.

"It's like a miniature Grand Canyon."

"Very miniature."

A set of rapids surprised us, sending our ship into chaos.

"Put your fucking weight in it!" Lee, looking back at each of us in turn. We were out of control, rocking wildly, a bag fell out of the raft then another. None of us could save them, all our energy was going into the oars; we didn't dare set them down.

We have no business out here. None of us know what we're doing...we're gonna roll or something.

But then rapids ended and the river widened. The canyon opened into another valley maybe a mile wide.

"How many rapids like that do we go through?"

Ben didn't respond. He looked confused, maybe a bit disturbed.

"I didn't even see that one on the maps. So...I don't know."

"Fucking great." Lee, setting her oar down to grab a beer.

"What did we lose?"

It only took Marcus a quick look to figure that out.

"Your shit, David...and the tent."

"Awesome."

"How long ago did Angela die, David?"

"Come on, Lee; stop being an asshole---"

"Just humor me."

I have to dig in my mind a bit, root down to where the information is buried.

"It will be a year on December 16th."

"So...six months. How have things been for you, Ben?"

"Uh, I lost my best programmer and my dog has cancer so...not so great."

"Marcus?"

"What?"

"Has your luck changed in the past six months? I bet it has," Lee continued. "One of my subcontractors fucked up and I got sued." She looked back at me.

"We know you're a mess."

"So...you're saying Angela was our good luck charm?"

"Or that spell she did protected us and it broke when she died."

'It was a fucking accident---"

"Maybe that's the worst part; it was just a stupid accident."

39

More drifting, more silence. It felt hotter than the previous days.
My sunscreen had been in that bag. Lee should have been drinking
water instead of beer but none of us were about to suggest that.

"We need to talk about things." Marcus, looking over at Lee,
probably dreading her reaction.

"What does talking do?" She shot a look back at me. "This place is
haunted, we found a fucking leg bone in the fire ring. Talking
doesn't change the fact that we will go through weirder and weirder
shit before this trip is through."

"I am still not sure how much of the first night happened. It
bothers me...does it bother any of you guys?"

"Yeah."

"You guys know me," Ben said. "I get high but I am still together; I
checked out all sorts of maps and this...those rapids weren't
supposed to be there. All this"---he gestured at our
surroundings---"is supposed to be different. Marcus, you saw the
river when we were driving back from the end point..."

"Yeah, yeah. It didn't look like this."

"Could we have taken a wrong fork or something?"

"*Branch* and no; I mean, do any of you remember a split?"

All of us muttered in the negative.

"I saw a little girl in the woods." Just blurted it out, yep.

Lee stared at me but then softened.

"That doesn't surprise me; wish it did."

She faced forward. Marcus reached down and got a bottle of water to hand to her.

"Drink some of this, it has to be close to a hundred."

Lee didn't take the bottle for the longest time.

40

Morning became afternoon on the second day:

"You're hitting that vape pretty hard. We may need you if we hit any more surprise rapids."

Ben looked over at me; had that come out wrong? Harsh? I smiled to let him know I was just poking fun. Looking at his face I saw fear. He was scared, laid back Ben, really scared despite the cushion of weed. That made *me* scared.

What do you know about this place that you haven't shared?

Ah, dude, no...I really don't...you guys really don't want me to go there...

"What?" Marcus had been watching us and picking up on Ben's anxiety.

And then Lee looked back.

"I don't believe in curses and ghosts so...I didn't take it seriously."

Ben was struggling to get the words out; maybe it was fear of our reaction or maybe it made his thoughts more *real* if he verbalized them.

"This area has a fucked up history. A major pioneer trail went through here. We all know what happened on pioneer trails---"

"Pioneers often died."

"Yeah, and when they died because of Indians the Army would come in and massacre the Indians. Ah, history---"

He reached down, rummaged for something, and pulled up an unopened bottle of whiskey.

"Most of the settlers died at their own hand, making stupid mistakes, getting lost. A couple of wagons were attacked by Indians in retaliation for a previous Army massacre. They were shot full of arrows then set on fire, kids included."

He looked at me: *There's your little girl, and the bone in the fire.*

"It came as a shock. The Indians had been allies, had saved scores of pioneers who fucked up and got lost of whatever---"

"It shouldn't have been a shock if the Army massacred them."

"Probably not," Ben took a long drink and then passed the bottle to me. "Anyway, the Army was sent in to teach the Indians a lesson. The unit or company or whatever got lost. Heat got to them, lack of food, rattlesnakes; it was just a fucked up trip for those Army dudes. They had a guide, one of the Indians. This Indian suggested they perform a ritual, smoke these wild herbs, sacrifice a deer..."

He trailed off. It took the rest of a few seconds to catch on to what he was saying.

"No way, this is bullshit." Lee plucked the whiskey bottle from where I had tossed it and took a long swallow.

Marcus was looking around. I could see a wildness beginning in him, his movements. He was fighting it, though, struggling to find peace with his logic and common sense.

"We need to stop this. This is how mass hysteria starts."

Our friend looked at each one of us in turn: *We need to calm the fuck down and stop feeding into our weird, fucked up fears and fantasties.*

"Those hipsters smoked us out with...I don't know drugs, some sort of hallucinogenic---"

"How did they remove every trace of their being there by early morning? *Why* did they do it?"

"Just...work with me, okay? We have to keep our heads."

"Maybe hard if ghost Indians attack." Yeah, I should have kept my mouth shut.

Marcus stared at me and shook his head.

"They're kids. They can probably party and still be on the water before our middle aged asses."

He was working so hard to guide us back to sanity that none of us wanted to point out all the holes in his very logical and rational and sane explanations.

The truth is, it was a mutual understanding that we were anywhere but a logical and rational and sane situation.

But Marcus needed that, so we gave it to him.

We would help him stay in that beautiful place as long as we could.

41

The whiskey was good but it was too hot and too early to be drunk.
The river arched into another wood. The shade from the canopy
felt good but---

*They could climb over those branches and drop right down on us. Who
knows what they'd do if they were in the boat.*

"I see some!" A boy's voice on the shore.

I didn't want to look: Would they be skeletons? On fire?

No, they were just two happy looking teenage boys, white shirts
and dark pants.

"Homespun," Ben muttered with a slight tremor to his voice.

We looked at each other. Bad idea: The fear in our eyes reflected,
bounced back and forth, gained strength.

The boys ran easily along the shore. I could see their bare feet
barely touching the ground, maybe not touching it all. They had
rifles, long rifles, one aimed at us as he ran.

"Holy fuck! They're gonna shoot at us!"

Marcus, dropping his paddle and ducking down.

"They can't hurt us, dude." Ben, sounding calmer than his eyes had
been,

"They're pointing rifles at us!"

Pops from the shore, smoke curling from one barrell. No whine of bullets coming our way, though, even if the rifle had been pointed right at us.

Lee had been rummaging in a bag and now had something in her hands and was pointing it---a gun, she had a gun and was aiming it like a cop in a movie.

After four shots she shook her head and put the gun back in its case.

"They're kids, Lee, it's probably best you missed, they're probably BB guns anyway---"

"I didn't fucking miss. I was looking down the barrel at both of them."

She hadn't missed and the boys hadn't missed even though it seemed as if I was looking down the barrel of *their* rifles--

The boys were still laughing and pointing us out.

Ghosts, I knew it, so did the rest of my friends---

Are you serious? Ghosts?? Come on, dude, this is still whatever the hipsters smoked us out with. Maybe it's still that first night and the four of us are tripping balls.

"They're climbing onto that tree down there."

"How did they get down there so fast?"

"Row, to the other side of the river, fucking row!"

Marcus, picking up his oar and rowing for his life---

Bad choice of words, dude, bad choice.

We got the raft as close to the other side as we dared but we would still be going right under the tree the boys were watching us from. They were laughing, bare feet dangling over where we would pass.

"Get your knife out!" One ordered. "They're almost under us."

"Shit, row to the shore!"

"Look at those rocks! If we puncture this thing we're stuck out here!"

And we were under the boys and they were dropping from the tree. I dropped my oar and raised my arms to protect myself; I wasn't alone in that.

Ash, that's what fell into the raft; ash with white chunks all of us would deny were bone fragments.

42

Further down the river Marcus was brushing his arms as he looked up.

"It *was* bone fragments." Lee, quieter than usual.

"And you know what human bone fragments look like?" Marcus, the pitch of his voice higher. Hysterics. He was getting hysterical.

"Da-v-id My-er! Pull up at the next beach, we have singing and music!"

"Fuck you, chinbeard!"

Was the Invisible Man bothered by Lee's insult?

"We all know it was bone fragments, not that it matters. Why did you have to be so stupid, David? You're not a stupid guy."

"Stop beating him up; it doesn't bring her back."

"I'm just frustrated---"

"You still love her; you're grieving." Ben, his voice musical.

"Fuck you." That, nearly inaudible.

43

Back on the second afternoon the forest thinned and the earth the trees grew out of lightened. The bark was gnarled, dry looking, as was anything sprouting out there. Even after the sun went over the hills it was still hot. Night was coming. None of us wanted to admit that or talk about it. We rowed in silence after the ash fell into the boat. Lee had some in her hair; none of us mentioned it. I kept seeing how white the skin on those boys looked, trying not to glance at their faces, what evil I might see there...or grinning skulls.

You're losing your shit. This is just a psychedelic trip gone bad; don't keep feeding it.

"We need to talk about this." Marcus, looking around at each of us in turn.

"No, we don't." Lee, of course. "If we talk about things we'll just see that we're seeing the same shit which means we're not tripping."

"We could be; come on Ben, the power of suggestion works when you're high, right? All of us could just be feeding each others' trips?"

Ben looked uncomfortable with our attention on him.

"Yeah, I've experienced it---"

"See!"

"--but, uh...never mind. We're probably just tripping balls, still."
Unconvincing. *Completely* unconvincing. The raft became silent
again aside from the sound of the water against the hull. Minutes
passed. It was starting to get dark; we needed to find a place to stop
for the night. I said as much.

"Maybe we should keep going."

"In the dark? It's completely black out here; we could run aground
or rip the fabric on something. If we fuck the raft up..."

If we fucked the raft up who knew how long it would take to walk
out---

And who knew what we would come across out there.

As if on cue: Laughter from the brush, it sounded like an older
man---yes, that was when we first heard the Invisible Man. There
were whispers of adult men and women; I tried to make out words
before realizing that I really didn't want to know what they were
saying.

"Still want to stop?"

"Let's get a mile or so further down the river."

44

"We have rope and a stake, maybe we could use that as an anchor."

"Won't work. We have to beach it."

Beach it. Strand ourselves on land. It would take minutes to get the raft free and away from the shore and whatever was waiting further inland. There was no choice, it was too dark to navigate and all of us were feeling the effects of drinking beer and whiskey.

"Sleep in the raft or on land?"

It was a stupid question. All of us would get as comfortable as possible in our corner of the boat. No one brought up starting a fire that night; maybe it was because we didn't want to gather wood or maybe it was because we didn't want to signal whatever was out there that we were beached---

Or maybe it would be another reminder of the bone in the firepit or the ash falling from that tree.

We ate jerky and tuna packets and other lazy snacks. I couldn't imagine falling asleep, just lying there unaware and vulnerable.

It hurts, maybe we should leave it alone.

Hold still. Stop being such a baby.

Angela, pulling the stitch from my head as she has done dozens or times.

And then holding the black thread with a single drop of blood that clings to one end before falling.

I wait for the string to twitch like some evil, living thing but it doesn't.

My wife is staring at the area on my head the string was pulled from, she looks---Disgusted? Confused? Worried? Yes.

"Oh, my God."

"What?!"

She pokes at my head with an index finger. There is the sound not unlike when you pull a boot out of the mud and a sensation....

Not pain, there should have been pain but there wasn't; just a slight tugging and then some tingling.

And then Angela was holding my scalp up for me to see. My scalp, my hair, no blood, though---

"When did this happen?"

I had no answer.

And then I was flying like a bird or a bat over where the raft was beached. Four people were asleep in it. I circled close, so close I could see there was still ash in Lee's hair. I was flying but I had no control over my course; circling close over the raft and then going higher and wider; seeing the people out there in the bush and the trees who were in turn watching the four people sleeping in the raft.

45

I awoke in the dark. The others were still asleep. The dream had dissolved the moment my eyes opened but I could still see it; the people all around us watching, waiting.

Calm down. It was a fucking dream. You're spooked, your imagination is running away from you, that's it.

Reassuring words, logical thoughts that should have provided comfort or at least a map back to calmness. They didn't.

I just lay there wrapped in my sleeping bag, shivering but not cold. My scalp was itching; I told myself it was fleas, *wanted* it to be fleas. It took forever for the first pink light to come over the ridge. Such a fucked up place but such beautiful light. It was mine for a few minutes before leaning over to push Ben.

"Hey, it's morning."

He didn't stir, the others hadn't been awakened by my voice. I shoved Ben harder. His head moved in a strange way, there was the sound of fabric ripping...

And his head rolled off and into the river.

"Holy shit! Lee! Marcus!"

Why were they not responding to my yelling and the sound of Ben's head rolling in the water? I crawled over our stuff towards them.

My friends were very still. And then...shapes, several arrows sticking out of each of them.

An awareness of people approaching. Indians, faces blank, leveling bows at me, preparing to fire arrows into my body.

46

Ben jumped back when I screamed. My eyes opened: It was morning. All three of them were alive. My outburst scared the crap out of them for a moment.

"Just...don't tell us, okay?" Lee, shaking her head and climbing out so we could free the raft. I pinched myself until I bled, needing to confirm that I was actually awake before joining the others in unbeaching the raft.

"What if we're dead."

"Just...stop that shit, dude. Please."

"Yeah, let's not use the 'd word;' not out here."

We drifted in silence. There was a current but it was mild. The water was so pure and clear you could see the bottom a few feet down.

"I'm sorry I fucked things up, guys."

"You already said that."

"Yeah, it's just..."

I trailed off but I couldn't trail off, one of us had to talk about something, something that wasn't whatever was going on with that river.

"I was shitty to you, Lee. That was my first fuck up. I know words mean nothing, apologies are useless, I just wanted to acknowledge that."

"You're right, apologies are useless." Her tone was hard. Ungiving. I could feel walls up around Ben and Marcus as well.

"To be fair to myself, it was an accident...you guys need to give me that."

Marcus looked at me shaking his head: *Just...none of us want to talk about this.*

"We're going into another canyon, probably rougher water."

I hadn't even noticed the valley growing narrower but now it was only a couple hundred yards across. Then maybe twenty yards. The river was descending---

Into Hell.

Not helping...not helping at all.

The raft became a toy shaken by an angry child: Nearly losing control, nearly losing bags, nearly flying into rocks.

And then we were becalmed. Wasted from our efforts we lay back and let the raft drift. The end came around but we didn't stop it. The water was calm, we were tired. The boat went around a bend.

"Fuck, we need to---"

We needed to steer around a rock but it was too late to react. The raft struck the boulder hard enough to send Marcus flying into the middle of the boat. I braced for the sound of the fabric tearing and the sensation of the raft deflating.

"We're stuck."

"Can we row out?"

"Probably not. It feels calm but there's still a current--"

Marcus had gotten back into his corner of the raft. He was looking over the side.

"Can you still see the bottom?"

"Yeah." His tone of voice was strange---had he *ever* used that tone of voice?

"How deep does it look?"

No answer. He hadn't moved, he was still leaning over, seeing something.

"What do you see?" Why did Lee have to ask that?

She had to, *one of us* had to.

Ben motioned for me to switch sides. On the same side of the raft as Marcus, he moved halfway up the boat and looked over.

"There's a woman down there."

"What? It's probably some driftwood or something."

"No...it's a woman in a long white dress. Looks like something out of a Victorian photograph or something."

"Come on, dude, you're full of---"

"No, he isn't." Marcus, with a gasp.

"Ah, fuck fuck fuck!" Ben, leaping back, his eyes screwed closed.

"What?!"

Ben hugged himself, eyes closed, struggling to make words.

"Her eyes opened." Marcus, way too calm. Shock? "She's smiling...smiling at me."

He smiled and waved at the lady ten or twenty feet below our raft. Lee grabbed Marcus and pulled him back. Ben and I had gotten into our original places without realizing it.

"We need to get out of here."

"How? We're stuck against the rock."

I didn't want to talk. I knew the answer but by sharing it I was, in effect, volunteering myself for the task.

"Two of us need to get in, push the raft away from the rocks while the other two work the oars."

"Fuck...I'll do it." Lee, starting to work her way back.

"Yeah, it's my idea so...me too."

"Wait: You guys want to get in the water with whatever that is right below?"

"Tell me what choice there is?"

Cowed by Lee who was now only a couple of feet from him, Ben raised his hands in supplication. I watched her bracing herself before clamoring over the side. I just jumped in with one hand on the side, felt my anchor hand slip---

And then I will go down and she'll come up and we'll embrace.

My anchor hand found the rope on the side. I made my way to the back, focused on working with Lee to push us from the rocks and free the raft---

Focused on not looking down.

Struggled to ignore the sensation--

That the lady was moving.

That she was coming for us.

I could hear Ben and Marcus struggling with the oars, yelling instructions at each other.

"We're getting clear! Okay, just hold on, we're moving!"

Ben's end of the raft was the back end again. Lee and I were getting pulled along. She climbed back in easily being much stronger than myself.

I was tired from the effort and still wearing shoes.

"Come on you pussy!" Lee, reaching a muscular arm over.

Slowly, with her help, I climbed back into the raft and we continued down the river.

First, though...

I will tell myself it was a submerged branch or we had gotten back into shallow water with a lot of large rocks.

That was it, that branch or rock, *that* was what bumped against my foot as I struggled back into the raft.

47

Further down the river:

Everyone looks at me.

It was just a branch.

This we agree on without words.

This we *have* to agree on.

48

The spell Angela cast took all night. My memory of it is poor, Ben had smoked us out. Most of the weed back then was shitty but he had gotten ahold of something powerful; even Marcus got really stoned.

Details are lost, maybe never stored.

Being the closest thing to the bad kid in our group, I had broken into a house that was for sale. We had done the ritual there; in the garage I want to say, using the concrete floor for chalking what I remember as a pentagram.

Was it a pentagram or am I remembering a movie?

Details are lost, maybe never stored.

The end of the night I have dreamed about a few times---has it always been a dream? It would have to be. All five of us crammed into Ben's BMW. Me in the back middle between Lee and Angela. Feeling their warmth, their thighs against mine, their breasts occasionally against my arms.

Sometimes the dream is just the five of us listening to music and talking and laughing like any other day.

Sometimes it ends with Ben muttering something and us colliding with another car.

The dream goes black there.

49

After freeing the raft from the boulders we just drifted.

None of that had happened; how could it?

The current breathed for a few minutes then stilled. There were just four people in a raft barely moving in the late morning warmth.

"All that rowing made me hungry."

"I almost forgot: I brought some rolls and there are cold cuts in the cooler."

"Cold cuts? You took space for beer with cold cuts?"

Laughter, even Lee smiled. How could they be acting so *normal*?

That's because none of that happened---how could it?

Those words were beautiful but meaningless. My friends were in shock; they couldn't deal with what we had experienced...what we *continued* to experience.

We made sandwiches. I wasn't sure I'd be able to eat but food just disappeared in my mouth. The four of us ate, the raft drifted, the sun rose higher in the sky. The water was still clear, you could still see the bottom; everytime I found myself staring over the edge of the raft, though, I would jerk back. My friends saw me do it but said nothing.

None of that happened, how could it?

"How much further, Ben? You said we're riding a hundred mile stretch?"

Maybe that question pushed him back into reality because he looked uncomfortable.

"Don't know, guess the maps I checked out were bunk. We got plenty of food, though. Marcus brought a water filter, Lee has a gun for hunting..."

The gun. Thinking about the gun meant acknowledging it had been fired at the boys which meant acknowledging the lady in the river---I saw all that on his face. Ben looked over the side of the raft, thought better of it, and fumbled for his vape pen. Up front, Lee and Marcus were passing a whiskey bottle back and forth. They were numbing themselves, just trying to ride this shit out. Literally.

What right did I have to take that from them?

None.

50

"That was right before we started hearing the Invisible Man."

"No, we heard him before then--"

"*Da-vid M-yer....you're almost here, keep rowin'!*"

"Great, you woke him up."

51

We left the canyon and entered another sparsely wooded area. The people on one side of the raft would row to keep their side furthest from land and then those on the *other* side would follow the same tactic; it took me an hour to realize that. Again, I said nothing, didn't even make a joke. Even a joke would have dragged reality back into the spotlight. It got hotter. The sounds of the insects changed with the heat. Sweat appeared on brows...

And the four of us were being watched.

Off to our left something was running among the bushes, a man shape.

Watching the shape, looking forward, realizing Lee had been watching me.

She nodded, faced forward again.

I'm not the only one who sees it.

"I think I saw a burger place at the other end," Ben said.

"Damn, a burger sounds good right now," Marcus sighed.

Voices a little bright, smiles a little too big. My friends weren't just in shock, they were fucked up. I kept thinking of how Marcus had waved at the lady in the water. I kept watching the man shape using my peripherals; he appeared to be an Indian, a brown man with dark hair nearly naked and carrying a bow---

What if my dream was about to come to fruition? What if we were minutes from an Indian attack?

Don't be an idiot. Remember what happened when the ghosts fired their ghost rifles? Like Ben said, they can't hurt you. Besides, all this is probably the lingering after effects of whatever was in that pipe. How many times do you need to be reminded of that?

"Hello! You there in the boat!"

A man was up ahead on the river bank, waving with his hat.

Homespun his clothes appeared, like the first man in the woods or the lady in the river.

"Dude looks like he needs help," Ben said. "Let's row over to the side."

Lee and I looked at each other. I could see we were on the same page: *Ben and Marcus are blocking out all the weird shit that has happened. They see this guy as just some local who is lost or something.*

We rowed over the bank. Marcus jumped out with the rope. The man had stopped waving; he was just standing there, smiling.

"Are you lost, sir? We have water if you need it."

The man said nothing, just stood there smiling.

"What is wrong with him?" Ben, quietly. "Maybe he's suffering from heat stroke or something."

His clothes...don't you guys realize that no one has worn clothes like that in over a hundred years?

Marcus was picking up on something; he tensed, took a step backwards.

The man just stood there, smiling. Saying nothing.

I could smell him now, the smell of campfires...and decay.

Marcus must have smelled it as well, he was pushing the raft back deeper into the river, climbing back into the raft without taking his off the stranger.

The man just stared, saying nothing, not moving.

Lee and I began rowing, working together to get us downstream and away from the silent stranger.

52

"That dude was dead."

No one responded to Ben, there was no need to--that dude *was* dead---

No, we can't give into this crazy shit. No. There is no such thing as ghosts or cursed rivers or any of that Scooby Doo shit---even in Scooby Doo there was always a logical explanation, Thelma ripping a mask off or something.

"Have you guys heard of that tea, the name is something like *euthenasia*? You completely lose touch with reality; it's so immersive and real you forget you are tripping. We may still be lying in our tent."

"No, this is real. I felt the sharp rocks cutting my feet on that last beach, I could *feel* that guy."

"*Feel* him? How?"

Marcus frowned. Clearly answering that question took him to a very bad place.

"He felt hungry, that's the best I can describe it."

"Like the lady in the river." Thanks, Ben.

"This can't be real..."

"It is fucking real!" Lee, clearly annoyed with all of us. "It shouldn't be, but it is. We all slip and out of denial but this shit is really happening. There are ghosts on this river---"

"Ghosts can't hurt us, at least."

"I don't know, they seem to be getting more and more real."

"That's because we're getting more and more freaked out."

"It's like they're feeding off that."

The four of us looked at each other.

"We need to be strong, not think about all the shit we've seen."

"Easier said than done."

"It has to be done," Marcus said firmly.

The four of us made a pact not to think about whatever we had seen on the river banks and the woods and especially not at the bottom of the river. If someone started slipping, they would ask for help and be forced to recount memories from our past. Before we pushed the raft into that fucking river. Hours passed. We felt less scared, I know I did. We had each other. The sun went over the mountains again.

"What about the river?"

"What about it?"

"Well, clearly something is not *normal* about it."

The three of us looked at Marcus: *Everything is fine, we can't go there, just focus on everything being normal.*

"Come on, dude; we're probably only a day away. I bet by this time tomorrow we'll be eating cheeseburgers and drinking beer out of glasses."

"Fuck you, pussies, I like beer out of a bottle," Lee growled.

Ben, Marcus, and I laughed at that

53

We found a decent beach before nightfall. Lee and Ben went to gather firewood while Marcus and I set up the fire ring.

"That dude was dead, I could fucking smell him."

I glanced around, expecting the silent stranger to walk out of the bushes nodding and smiling and pulling something sharp from his belt, something very real...

No. Pull him back.

"Marcus, he wasn't real. We're seeing shit out here. If anything was real, why didn't those bullets hit us?"

He just stared into the half finished fire ring. My friend was seeing the lady in the water again, I felt him tightening and sending off erratic shards of energy.

"What did you tell me when I started dating Andrea?"

No response. His hands were shaking a little.

"What did you say to me when I hooked up with Lee?"

"If you hurt her, I will kick your ass."

Marcus looked up at me, anger mixing with his fear--a step in the right direction?

"Right. So...how come you didn't kick my ass?"

My friend started moving rocks from a pile we had collected to finish the ring.

"The question is why did you have to test me like that? Why has it always been about *David*? Everything is always about you, dude."

Man, he was *grinding* those rocks into place---at least he didn't look scared anymore.

"Yeah, I fucked up. That is why I was surprised when Ben emailed me."

"He emailed you because I gave him no choice."

"Why did you want me here?"

Marcus passed the rock he had picked up between his hands; I half expected him to bash me in the skull with it.

"You're my friend. Maybe I can never accept that I would pick a shitty person to be my friend...I mean, what does that make me?"

The others were back with wood. Neither looked scared. I assumed that they had seen nothing.

54

"Oh, Dav-id M-yer! Isn't it a beautiful day! It'll be night soon."

Yes, it will be.

I am remembering as Marcus built the fire pit last night---he is silent now as are the rest of my friends. *It'll be night soon.* Yes, and we all know that this is the night when things get a lot more real. Maybe it was me that had brought the ghosts back into our life by killing Angela...

Old ghosts, new ghosts, it didn't matter---*ghosts.*

When she died the walls that had been protecting us had been knocked down.

Or, maybe I have made them real; a haunted person being a magnet for a haunting. Some people never move forward from the past. Some people, instead of choosing the living, they choose to spend their lives with ghosts. As the Invisible Man called out, I began to understand what I needed to do. Oh, it was terrifying at first---still is---but those first moments...

My mind drifted back to the previous night.

55

Coyotes howled in the distance as we sat around the fire drinking.
It could have been like any of the times the five of us had gotten
together in the future---
Five, now four. Yeah, things were the same and yet they clearly
weren't. Marcus had forced the others to invite me. Maybe we had
fallen back into being friends again due to our collective past or
maybe Ben and Lee were just tolerating me.
Maybe I can never accept that I would pick a shitty person to be my
friend...I mean, what does that make me?
Human.

"Walk with me." Lee, clearly not going to accept a *no*.
We left the others and headed out into the bush.
"It's cold out here," I said, nervous about her singling me out.
"It will get warmer, just walk."
We did. In silence. The area was very desert-like once we left the
trees near the river; mormon tea bushes and yuccas and white earth
like talcum. The two of us walked in silence. Lee clearly had
something to say, something to get out; I needed to just be
respectful and keep my mouth shut and wait for her to speak. We

climbed a slight rise. There was a manzanita at the top. Lee sat beneath it and I sat next to her. She shut off her headlamp and I did the same.

"Thank you," she said.

"What? Why would you thank me?"

She stared out into the darkness.

"For getting me past being a nice person."

I laughed, I couldn't help it.

"Why are you laughing?"

"Lee...that's ridiculous; what do you mean by that?"

She looked over at me. Even in the darkness I could feel her *hardness.*

That's the best word for her toughness, it was like a ring of burl around a tree; a toughness grown out of an injured thing.

That is what she is telling you with her hardness: You hurt her and she became an asshole.

"This world sucks, David. People are either weak and petty or strong and capricious. Phil is the one person I let in, because we all need one person. One."

"What about Ben and Marcus?"

"They're my buddies---you think I count on them for anything important?"

There was nothing I could say to that.

"Phil is my one person. Angela was yours. She loved you. You guys getting together...that *sucked* for me at first, but the two of you made sense. Besides, the sex thing between us didn't work for me."

"No?"

"Sorry, dude," she looked in the general of my shorts and smirked. It wasn't a playful smirk, it was a knife out smirk.

"You couldn't see what you had and you'll never have it again. I'm not angry at you, I feel bad for you. I feel sorry for you."

"Dude...do you think I chose that? Don't you think I fucking regret that every day?"

Silence. She stood up and switched her light back on.

"You're weak, but you're the only one who has to live with that, suffer that."

Lee started walking back towards the river. I gave her a few seconds before switching on my light and following.

56

I sat in my corner of the raft thinking about the things Lee said; harsh things, probably true things. At least they distracted me from the ghosts, *other ghosts*, ghosts I didn't own or control. Were the others thinking about what we had seen and perceived? Asking would have been throwing open a door, adding to my list of crimes. Lee and Angela had been together, I had wormed my way in and then had forced Lee out. She had loved Angela deeply, me less so...and then she had to be on her own but still around us.

Lee never stopped loving Angela. She says that Phil is her *One* but if Angela hadn't died and had decided to leave me?

Sleep remained just past the tips of my fingers. I listened to the water, pulled my sleeping bag closer as the chill became nearly violent.

"Are we feeling good?" Ben, as the raft began floating the next morning.

We looked at him for meaning. It took a few moments to read between the lines: *Are any of us thinking about all the fucked up shit out here?*

"I think so." Marcus smiled. "We're probably just a few hours away from those cheeseburgers."

"Fuck yeah." Lee nodded, muscles changing shape as she rowed.

There was a man shape up ahead in the trees. I immediately looked down, began focusing on my talk with Lee---

Marcus was looking in the direction of the man shape and then pointedly looking away. Ben wasn't, he was breaking our pact; I was just glad it wasn't me. The man shape came out of the brush to walk on the bank just ahead of us. An older man, clean shaven and wearing a frock coat. He looked delighted to see us but said nothing.

"You're not real, get the fuck out of here."

Lee's words had no effect on the stranger.

"Who brought this?" Marcus, looking at all of us accusingly.

And the stranger was fifty yards ahead of us---how had he moved so fast?

Because he's a ghost.

No, because he's not real.

The man in the frock coat stepped off the bank and into the water ahead of us, right in our course.

"Row to the right, row to the right!" Ben was scared, probably also feeling guilt for manifesting the stranger.

"No." Marcus, trying to shake off his fear and be firm. "He is not real, we'll go right through him."

As if that wasn't bad enough. Marcus was right, though, we'd probably just go right through the man in the frock coat just as Lee's bullets had gone through the boys with the rifles. The stranger put his arms out in front of him. Ben was still trying to row to the other side of the river, so I gave him a hard look.

"Dude, we're only seeing him because you're letting him in. He's not real---"

And then the stranger stopped the raft, stopped it as easily as if it were a small stick floating along and not a several hundred pound raft.

"I'm as real as any of you!" the stranger laughed, clearly delighted.

"What do you want?" Marcus, I could see him shaking some.

The stranger started singing some song about *gathering at the river*. Other voices joined him from the bushes, other male voices along with women and children. I screwed my eyes closed and hugged myself. Something changed...motion, the singing beside me and then behind me. The stranger had let us go.

No, he had let us go *for the moment*.

57

"That was the Invisible Man back there this morning. The voice, it's the same."

Marcus, not rowing, just miming with the oar a couple of inches above the water. A character in a play.

"You're right, David, I still love Angela," Lee said out of nowhere. "I wouldn't leave, Phil, though; I am not a shitty person."

Not a shitty person like you. I debated bringing up her fucking the beardo but it felt petty. It *was* petty, Lee wouldn't have done that if clear-headed. My friends were silent. They understood that there weren't any cheeseburgers waiting for them, no end to the trip. The ghosts would get stronger, more real; they would stop the raft and sing or just stare up from the bottom of that river.

"I know what I need to do."

No one responded. No one was moving, we were just drifting. There was barely any current. The water was smooth as a mirror. And the sun was leaving over the mountains.

"One of us needs to walk inland."

Lee looked back at me, uncomprehending. Marcus looked back; I could see he understood.

"What's going to happen to them?"

We were getting too close to shore. I rowed a couple of strokes to get us back in the weak flow.

"It's not what happens to them, it's what happens to the other three."

"A sacrifice." Ben, softly, through smoke.

All of us looked at him. Maybe it *had* been him that had brought the ghosts---he *looked* haunted.

"That's great, David." Lee, facing forward, shaking her head.

"We need to get closer to shore, I need to get off," I said.

"Don't be an idiot, dude."

"I'll take water. If this doesn't work...I'll walk out of here. There have to be roads out there."

"Roads are gone, dude; there's only the river and *them*."

I looked over at Ben. Where there had been a sort of soft-focus fondness there was just a blank. I looked at Marcus and Lee for signs of the closeness we had shared in the past: Blank. Blank.

I filtered four liters of water and put them in a backpack. If things work out the way I believe they will, the water will be superfluous. We pulled the raft close to shore and I climbed out. The water was cold, colder than it had a right to be. Climbing onto the bank I saw the people in the raft staring at me; what I was doing had no meaning to them, I could see that on their faces. That hurt but I understood that I was to blame, I had caused this. It was the shock of everything they had experienced. Maybe they will get it when they reach the end of the trip, when they are at that bar Marcus and Ben are drinking cold beers and eating cheeseburgers...

Maybe then they will see me as their friend again.

No, that cannot be why I have done this. Wanting that reaction---to be important to my three friends again---would be selfish. I need to be selfless, for once.

A path led away from the water and into the brush. I have been following it for maybe ten minutes with no idea where it leads but understanding that I am not lost. The three people in the raft stared at me for a few moments, then put to the oars and continued downstream. Part of me had wanted at least one of them to protest, to try and talk me into staying in the raft.

Wanting that was selfish---I need to be selfless, for once.

There is music up ahead: Men, women, and children singing. A fiddle player. Singing and laughter. Maybe I will join them. Maybe they will welcome me and I will become one of them.

Or maybe they will fall on me like vengeful spirits and tear me apart.

I have no idea.

All I know is that I have lived in this skin and only in this skin for too long. I have thought of others only in words and not in deed or spirit. As I walk I am thinking of that dream, Angela pulling the top off my head. She was always trying to get in there, always telling me how I kept so much from her. And I would protest: *No, I talk all the time, I tell you everything*. But that wasn't the truth. I was never giving, I was never truly open, I failed to share the best of myself, the most beautiful stuff. Everything that meant anything. And now I will.

The strangers are close now. I hear clapping along to what sound like church songs.

Fear comes like little sparks floating towards dry grass but I will continue walking. I will open myself up, I will accept what comes in the hope that my friends will reach their destination.

plop (die Natur ruft) plop (die Natur ruft) plop (die Natur ruft) plop (die Natur ruft)

plop (die Natur ruft) **Plop** plop (die Natur ruft) plop (die Natur ruft) plop

(die Natur ruft) plop (die Natur ruft) plop (die Natur ruft) plop (die Natur ruft) plop
(die Natur ruft)
plop (die Natur ruft) plop (die Natur ruft) plop (die Natur ruft) plop (die Natur ruft)
plop (die Natur ruft) plop (die Natur ruft) plop (die Natur ruft)
plop (die Natur ruft) plop (die Natur ruft)
plop (die Natur ruft) plop (die Natur ruft)
plop (die Natur ruft)

plop (die Natur ruft) plop (die Natur ruft)

plop (die Natur ruft) **(Nature Calls)**

plop (die Natur ruft)

plop (die Natur ruft) plop (die Natur ruft)

plop (die Natur ruft)

plop (die Natur ruft)

January 26th

There was too much sauce on my Carl's Catch today; it oozed out of the sides of the bun when I took a bite.
Yesterday was perfect, not too much and not too little.
Perfect is rare.

Started taking notes for this blog while eating lunch.
I always eat at my desk instead of the break room.
My cubicle walls are covered with pictures I've taken a shine to.
The newest one is a watercolor of a horse in mid-prance that my niece sent me.
That horse looks so proud, so lifelike.
I spent half my lunchtime marveling at that painting as I ate.
Even the sauce falling out of my sandwich couldn't distract me--
In my mind I was eating a fancy meal in a famous art gallery.

If you eat at your desk you run the risk of being interrupted.
It seems everyday someone is leaning in with a work question.
I mention it, but it doesn't bother me.
Everyone is nice where I work; we all talk and have a good time.
It always tickles me when my co-workers are interested in my pictures.

There is a story behind every one and I love sharing them.

Our office just got remodeled.
There's something reassuring about the smell of new paint and carpet.
The only flaw is that the nearest bathroom is closed for repair.
I asked my boss 'why' but she just made a face.
Wonder what's up with her.

Every couple of months we have mandatory overtime.
The assignments are written on a board in colored chalk; our department is yellow.
Some people make a fuss but I've never felt the need to complain.
I'll talk about my arthritis or the backaches I get but not that.
If a day seems long I just focus on my pictures of horses and dogs.
My wall calendar is open to the cutest picture of some Doodle puppies.
Before the horse picture came it was my favorite--I'd just sit there and imagine their puppy breath and how warm they'd feel if you held them.
Dogs are amazing, how they radiate love as long as you are kind to them.

Away from work I lead a pretty quiet life:

My husband Joe and I have had our house in Citrus Heights for over twenty years.

We have three dogs, all mutts.

Both of us are huge Rolling Stones fans; saw them on the Steel Wheels tour.

I'm close to my mother: She lives in Hawaii and I visit her twice a year.

She's 84 now and broke her left hip a couple of months ago---

I worry about her a lot because she doesn't have anyone on her island.

Talking to her about moving in with us is pointless; she won't even *discuss* leaving Hawaii.

My mother thinks my starting this blog is a waste of time—it is one of the few things we disagree on.

A couple of months ago I joined an online Group.

I worried about fitting in but have already made a few friends.

Before meeting them I wouldn't have believed that you could feel close to people you've never met in person.

I don't think we'll ever meet face to face, that would probably be awkward.

Looks like it's going to be just me and the dogs again.

Joe isn't home yet; he's probably doing something with his buddies.

That's the story most nights.

Joes tells me that they "do guy stuff" like work on cars.

He'll help them with *their* cars but won't even change my oil.

It seems like every night he's off helping someone with a lube job

or turning their rotors; I have to go to Jiffy Lube.

Our house has three-bedrooms, it was the perfect size for us and

the kids. Now that they're gone one room has become Joe's den and

another is the guest room is where I write this blog. We rarely have

anyone stay over, it's been months since I turned down the bed.

There is a big bottle of water on the desk that's always at least half

full.

My goal is to pee clear by the middle of the afternoon.

I'm proud to say that today I have met that goal.

Clean urine is a sign of good health, no one wants smelly yellow

urine.

Loadstar shared some new pictures with the Group today and they

were beautiful.

I could barely conceal my jealousy and I'm sure I wasn't alone.

We all oohed and ahhed over the photos in chat:

"That's a beaut!" Posted 10SegSteve.

"I'll say it is." Posted BrownGail

"The coloring is amazing." Posted NugPride

"Look at the point, that point is perfect!" Posted Loafman

"And the segmentation—it's *symmetrical*." Added 10SegSteve.

"A genuine work of art," was my comment.

Six comments; most shares are lucky to get four or five.

I got three one time and am working to double that.

Loadstar responded to each comment with a gold medal emoji.

He is a bit of a showboat but his bio says he's still in college—at that age it's easy to let things go to your head.

I haven't had anything to contribute to the Group in awhile and feel like a tourist. Last week I shared a really good picture and got two nice comments that had me walking on clouds for a couple of days but that was last week.

Last week was perfect.

Perfect is rare.

January 31st

It has been said that practice can make anything a habit.

My goal is to write in this blog every afternoon but it slips my mind.

Joe has been grumpy the past couple of days: He grumbles and grumbles like an old bear. I hear him shouting swear words when he's on the alone throne.

He would be sore if he knew I shared this, but I found streaks on his undershorts. Not just poo---there's *always* poo skids on his undershorts---but blood.

I'm guessing he has hemorrhoids.

Someone from my Group suggested something naughty but I put that dirty talk to rest.

It's just hemorrhoids---I said that to them and I also told myself that after I signed out of the Group.

It's just hemorrhoids.

There was too much sauce on my Carl's Catch again.

Every day I request light sauce but half the time the sandwich is drowning in it.

I think it's a tasty sauce but a little goes a long way.

In the middle of eating Yolanda brought me something that she needed help on.

I couldn't say no so my Carl's Catch got cold and my fries got soggy.

Fast food may be tasty when it's warm but cold it's as nasty as that Family Guy show my kids love.

Yolanda is the manager of our department and she's a skinny thing.

That girl is always rushing, always bent forward as she walks with a serious expression on her face.

She's in her mid-thirties and married with two small children.

I imagine she's a stranger to those kids because she works from eight to eight plus mandatory overtime five days a week.

Whenever I try to chat with her she always has to hurry off---

In my mind, that's no way to live.

You have to slow down and smell the roses.

You have to appreciate the little moments in life because one day you'll be old and grumpy and leaving blood streaks in your undershorts.

Just got back from Yolanda's office.

Should be working but wanted to write this down before forgetting it.

I walked into my boss's office and she asked me to close the door.

My supervisor, hunched over, more wrinkles than I had noticed before.

"Louise, I need your help," she said.

I smiled and nodded but was still confused about the closed door.

Yolanda swore me to secrecy, made me put my hand up and everything.

Once the pact was sealed she explained why the nearest bathroom is closed.

According to my boss, someone answered the call of nature on the floor and in the tank of the toilet.

"They call it a top loader, Louise---I looked it up."

A *top loader*: The Internet has given everything a name.

Yolanda asked me to keep an eye on the bathrooms--

She okay'd me spending more time in there if it helped her catch Miss Top Loader.

I told my boss that she could count on me in the bathroom.

Seeing Yolanda all bent over reminds me of my own back ache.

Following the dogs around every night to pet them means being hunched over a lot. They won't stay in place: All three pace restlessly, watching for Joe. We all do.

Moe found something in the garage and has been chewing on it---

Some chew toy, maybe Joe bought it.

It's a weird looking thing, thought it was a big rubber snake at first but made out of pink latex.

I'll put up a pic of it later and anyone who knows what it is can comment.

The Group is still buzzing about the pictures Loadstar submitted last week.

Even when not in the Group room I keep going back to it.

It's a thing of beauty: The points, the segmentation, the coloring.

I had a share recently and it was pretty good but nothing compared to Loadstar's.

Got one comment: Bravo. Bravo---hardly worthy of a gold medal emoji.

None of us have come close this week, his picture was perfect.

Perfect is rare.

There's a new fellow in my Group and I don't think I like him.

I can tell that he thinks we're all a big joke because he's always making wisecracks.

Even his screen name---DrFudge---sounds like he's having a laugh at our expense.

The day before yesterday he shared his first picture and the reaction was immediate:

"No soup! This isn't a soup site!" 10SegSteve posted.

"And stay away from the Fibercon!" BrownGail added.

Even a troll gets two comments.

DrFudge became very apologetic but it was easy to see through his act.

His share was removed from the board but I kept a screenshot of it.

DrFudge's submission is ugly and formless with what appears to be straw in it---

It's just an awful mess of a thing but I keep looking at it.

I see the jpg sitting on my desktop and feel compelled to open it...

Maybe I am nasty, too.

Maybe I am as nasty and ugly and malformed as DrFudge's creation.

No angles, no segments, just a blob.

February 3rd

My Carl's Catch was too dry today.
You'd think they'd train their cooks to get the perfect dollop on but
I guess there's no such thing.
Some folks probably like a lot of sauce and some like it dry; I like it
somewhere in between.

Yolanda came by my cubicle as I ate.
Her suit looked rumbled and there were dark circles under her
eyes.
My boss glanced around for eavesdroppers before leaning in.
"Have you seen anything, Louise? In the bathroom?"
She looked so worried and serious that I almost hugged her.
"What's up?" I asked.
Another glance in every direction for people who weren't there.
"It happened in the other bathroom."
The sandwich wrapper teased between my fingers, thin paper on
skin---
Wondering what stories my face was telling.
"Was it another top loader thingee?"
Yolanda looked confused and then disgusted.
"No. God...no. But someone did their business on the floor and
wrote something on the wall."

My eyes met hers; I had never noticed what beautiful eyes my boss has.

"Wrote something?"

Yolanda looked at me as if she had the biggest secret in the world and wasn't sure if she could trust me with it.

"I think it was supposed to be a smiley face."

Yolanda leaned in close enough for me to smell her laundry soap and perfume along with her sweat.

They say that animals can smell fear.

"I can't close two bathrooms, Louise, it'd be an OSHA violation."

Another look around. She looked as frazzled as I felt at peace.

"I really need your help with this---maybe you can use the bathroom more often. If you need me to help with your workload I'll do it; this is the big fire this week."

Unwrapping my sandwich, aware of the power to end the conversation.

"You can count on me."

Joe and I had a spat last night. We don't have them very often---mostly we stay out of each other's way---but last night's beat the band.

Part of me wants to keep this blog lighthearted but I need to talk about this.

The fight took place in the kitchen, I was cooking and my husband was getting water.

I made a wisecrack about his goatee and saw Joe stiffen.

His face looked as if I were a stranger that had called him a name on the street.

He was an arm's length away and there was the smell of a new cologne---

It reminded me of our date nights long ago.

The coldness in his eyes, however, reminded me of where we are today and that there probably won't be any more nights on the town for us.

My husband walked sternly out of the kitchen to use the computer.

From the guest room came a cry of surprise and an obscenity.

I understood what had happened: The computer was still logged in as me and Joe had found my jpgs.

A rush of cold and an instant upset stomach knowing it was my duty as a wife to go in there and confirm what Joe had found.

Forcing myself to walk down the hall tail between my legs.

Standing an arm's length away like a prisoner awaiting a sentence.

Joe snapped cruel things at me like a shoe to the ribs.

Turning back to the computer, my husband selected the pictures and pressed down on the delete key with his thumb--

It was like he was killing a pest.

My fear turned to anger and mean things came out of my mouth.

Remembering how to yell and how good it feels to yell---

Barking things I can't accept.

Joe's response was that I don't understand him or what he feels.

It felt like the pot calling the kettle black seeing as he doesn't understand who *I am*, who I *really* am.

Both of us have found things that are important to us that the other can't understand.

Hopefully those things won't cause us to ever stop being married.

I still have love for Joe and the house we have shared for over twenty years.

You don't switch horses this late in life, you just buck up and stay the course.

I keep seeing how disgusted Joe looked when he saw the jpgs on my desktop.

I've seen that face in the mirror--

Accepting what makes me tick took years.

Curly was a puppy when I began to understand what I need, now she's got gray on her muzzle and I'm just starting to feel okay.

All those years of feeling like a bad person, a dirty person.

I felt guilty and ashamed like I was doing something wrong and ugly.

I also understood that this is who I am and have to accept it.

The Group helped me: Finding other good people who have this sort of interest has made it easier for me to feel okay again.

That feeling is still written hesitantly on a chalkboard.

My husband stormed in and wiped the words off in a rage.

It has left me feeling like a loyal dog that got a swift kick it didn't deserve:
I was good, offering only love and staying when others would have left.

When I was using the potty after lunch Yolanda used the stall next to me, I knew it was her from the sound of her heels.
She started grunting up a storm and all these loud sounds came out of her.

Such a big noise from such a skinny thing---a big noise and a big smell: Sometimes nature calls in a big voice.
Yolanda was there for eleven minutes--
I shuffled my feet and made the noises you make on the toilet until she flushed and left the bathroom without washing her hands.
I'll definitely hold her next memo by the corner.
I went into the stall as the currents were dying in the toilet.
There was a small brown streak in the bowl that looked like a question mark

February 8th

Yesterday I was able to rewrite some words on my chalkboard.

DrFudge, I didn't know you read this; thank you for your kind words.

Your words of support and encouragement mean a lot to me.

The lima bean casserole sounds like a winner; will try it soon.

Last night I was cooking broccoli and navy beans when nature called:

A familiar weight moving through me.

Just enough time to grab the special light I use for my pictures.

My share had a lot of pebbling but the color was good and there was a strong crescent ending on a point.

Got four comments from the Group including a really nice one from Loadstar.

Despite drinking sixty ounces of water my urine remained deep yellow and pungent.

It felt like I had to pee all day---can drinking so much water strain your bladder?

Back to your comments DrFudge:

Yes, I *am* serious: I have no idea what Moe has been chewing on.

Now Curly has been fighting her for the toy and those dogs never fight.

Moe is the worst; she won't let the Thing out of her sight.

That dog is either licking at it or carrying it off to hide it.

It's so long it sways when she runs with it.

Now Curly is snarling at Moe and having a tug of war over the Thing.

They were squabbling over it as I tried out a special brownie recipe last night.

Joe came into the kitchen to grab a bottle of water when I was cooking.

He had no interest in the brownies or talking to me.

Moe and Curly were fighting over the mysterious chew toy next to the dishwasher.

Joe watched them while I stirred in the sugar, saw a scowl make his face ugly.

My husband growled about the dogs, accusing me of not keeping them in line.

When I asked what he meant he just looked frustrated.

I know that face, it's the "You're stupid, Louise" face.

Joe started squeezing his water bottle so hard it should have burst.

He wanted to say something, could almost see the words forming in his mouth.

My husband stomped away before they could come out.

I ate most of the brownies hot but a couple were left over for work this morning. I made sure they were hidden whenever anyone came by my cubie. One of the gals leaned in and said that she smelled something good. Thought about sharing them, I think she saw my hand moving toward the drawer.

Understanding it could lead to trouble, my hand stopped.

My co-worker looked disappointed when I smiled and suggested that the smell was coming from another cubicle.

Yolanda needs a vacation. She has been pacing as she talks to herself---

Her suits are wrinkled and her hair isn't as tidy as it used to be.

My boss keeps looking over at the bathroom and shaking her head.

This morning she was arguing with the janitor in the parking lot.

Most of it was Spanish talk, but seven words were in English:

"There's only so much I can do."

On my first break I went into the kitchen to get some coffee.

Two gals from HR were talking about the bathroom.

One sounded afraid and I don't understand that at all: If only she could see things as they really are.

Nothing happened last night or this morning—was there a mistake with the brownie recipe?

By lunchtime I was ready to mark it off as a failed experiment.

On the way to Carl's Junior, however, the brownies finally kicked in.

Had the Stones on the stereo and understood that I had roughly three songs to reach a bathroom...

Two, if one of the songs was Gimme Shelter.

Shifting in my seat, holding my legs together, wondering---

What if I just pulled off next to a park and let nature happen?

What if I just soiled myself as I sat in the front seat?

Children would wave from the park; I'd smile and wave back as I sat there in my own filth.

It'd be squishy and dirty; chances are it'd leak through my jeans and stain the seat.

Joe would see the stain and say ugly things and I'd say ugly things back.

The thread holding everything together would finally snap.

No, I didn't want that.

There was a space in the WalMart parking lot close to the doors.

My guts had knotted up and felt full of liquid.

Hurrying past men's wear, I wasn't sure if I was going to make it---

What if I had a bad accident next to the bargain DVD bin?

Would it stay in my underwear or would it run all the way down to my shoes?

Probably the latter; I could tell what I was holding in was mostly liquid.

Would the Arab looking man poking through the bargain DVDs notice?

Would the smell of my impatient bowels distract him from buying *When Harry Met Sally* for $3.99?

I wanted to stop right there and let it happen.

Just letting go right there as that dark skinned stranger stared at me.

Doing so would have meant going home to change my clothes:

I'd be late getting back from lunch and Yolanda would be mad---

What if I went back to work like that?

What if I went back with my Carl's Catch and fries like any other day but with nasty jeans?

Maybe I'm a coward because I kept walking towards the bathroom.

The songs had ended, it was time to find a seat.

Struggling to keep things in, making my legs go faster.

Worried I wouldn't make it, finding the door, shoes slapping on tile.

The release was enormous and frightening at first.

Fearful, struggling to remind myself that I was where I was suppose to be---

Hitting a peak, stabbed with spasms, a hurtful sort of bliss.

Explosion. Rest. Spasm. Explosion.

A minute passed with my eyes closed.

The seat was warm beneath me, my breath slowed, and peace found me.

It grew so quiet my blood sounded like lazy waves moving up a beach.

Someone walked in the bathroom and gagged.

"My word, do you need an ambulance?" It sounded like an older woman.

All the weight was gone, all my strength, even making two words was a chore.

"I'm fine."

She walked out.

When the movement ended the euphoria passed, everything drained.

DrFudge, it felt as if the bones had been removed from my legs; it took a few seconds to stand up.

The floating toilet paper reminded me of angels.

I pulled my phone from my purse, opened the stall door to get better light.

Took two pictures and emailed them to myself.

Looked from the phone to the bowl and back to my phone.

It was a truth that had not been allowed to be told; flushing it would have been a tragic denial.

My Carl's Catch had just the right amount of sauce.

Also, an onion ring was mixed in with my fries---it had been a good day. Yolanda interrupted my lunch but I didn't mind, small things

couldn't touch me. My boss was holding out a folder and saying things; I smiled and nodded but it was just my body doing it---
My thoughts were in the stall I had used at Wal-Mart, imagining someone discovering what I had left behind.
If only they could appreciate the very personal moment we will be sharing; something quiet yet powerful. We're all connected, the things we do affect many other lives. Our actions, even the easy ones, have meaning and importance.
Even when we feel small and alone we touch people.

February 11th

DrFudge: I'm embarrassed knowing that you've been reading this, that you know I look at your picture all the time.
Such an ugly mess with pieces of what look like straw---no form, no texture, no geometry.
It's ugly but—
I keep opening that jpg many times a day.
Joe thought he deleted it but he underestimates me.
I hope you are not upset that your comment was deleted. I appreciate your input on what the chew toy really is...
Maybe you're right, maybe you're wrong, I just can't go there.
Not today, maybe not ever.

My pee was still bright yellow when I went to cook supper.
Dehydrated; have to be careful with that brownie recipe in the future.

Another night of dinner for one: Joe was out somewhere, maybe with his friends who work on cars, who knows. He has started wearing Kenneth Cole shirts to go with his expensive cologne and goatee. I don't know why he had to change, the old Joe worked so well for me. I've read that married couples can grow apart: People change or just get bored and men have midlife crises. Joe is almost sixty so I think it's too late for that sort of thing.

I think that but how else do you explain it?

The articles I've read on the Web give me answers I'd rather die than accept.

I think of those articles when looking in the mirror---

My blouses come from Ross or Marshall's and no one gives me a second look.

Maybe this thing with Joe is partially my fault.

There was quite a fuss at work on Friday:

Someone did their business all over one of the toilets in the ladies room. There was a lot of fuss, a lot of squawking, and I just sat back and listened. I felt like Mick Jagger probably does when he eavesdrops on people leaving one of his concerts.

That's so gross! Seriously---who would s*** all over the toilet?!

Not just the toilet; it's all over the floor, too!

Sitting in my cubicle, eyes closed, feeling warmth rush through me. Pride. Glory. All the worries about Joe gone, at least for a couple of minutes.

The music of voices was all around me. With the swell of it came an understanding like small, brown birds moving through the air with sticks for a nest.

There is love for me, even if at times it has seemed cruelly repossessed---

It's out there somewhere, swirling like dust, and if I close my eyes and open myself to it that love will find me.

I tell myself that as often as I open your jpg, DrFudge.

Thank you for the Happy Valentine's Day wishes, DrFudge. Aside from your kind words this hasn't been a good day.

Caught Joe in the garage dancing to "Anybody Seen My Baby" by the Stones. He turned red and barked at me for walking in without knocking. We just stood there staring at each other as the song played. I wasn't about to cry in front of him, he wouldn't care anyway.

What happened to those days when he'd do silly dances for me? He'd do them and we'd laugh and have a fine time.

The song became muffled when I closed the garage door and went to make another dinner for one.

I was logged into the Doodle community when I got your message, DrFudge. The picture you attached confused me at first; I thought it was a close up of refried beans. I should have recognized it but I thought it was taken down weeks ago.

How did you find it, DrFudge?

Seeing it reminded me of when I learned my place in the Group and what I could and could not share. That experience was like a bite from a dog that fools you with kind eyes.

That picture was the real me, *is* the real me.

A reminder of all the things I have been taught I can never share.

The links he sent remain unopened; that picture is enough for now.

February 15th/16th

It is midnight. In six hours I will wake, put on my work clothes and
work smile and leave here.

Will there be sleep between now and then? I'm not sure.

Joe and I had another spat tonight. He grabbed the chew toy from
Curly and tossed it in the garbage. My husband was rough with my
dog so I spoke up. He snarled and pulled the thing from the trash,
one end was ragged.

"Where are the balls, Louise?"

Of all the words last night those five, in that sequence, stand out.

Why couldn't you have been wrong, DrFudge?

The two of us stood on either end of the kitchen island squabbling.

I don't see the point in rehashing every word of the fight; they were
the same ones we've used dozens of times.

All but those five in that sequence: *Where are the balls, Louise?*

Joe talked about what had become a chew toy; it seemed like he
needed to.

Talking about it seemed mean at first but then I understood.

Big Bob the Bloodletter, that's the name my husband and his
friends gave the toy---guess that explains the stain I found in Joe's
shorts.

I told him that I had been afraid he had cancer or something.

Both of us chuckled at that and then everything got quiet...neither of us knows where to go from here.

We were raised to see marriage as a sacred bond that you don't break.

Mom reminded me of that during our last talk on the phone:

You don't just change horses in midstream, you buck up and stay the course.

She knows about the chew toy, DrFudge.

Mom knows about it, knew what it was, and called Joe a bad name.

In the next breath she reminded me that we have to stay together, even if we are two strangers leading two lives in one house.

Around ten we ran out of words and Joe left the house. I sat on the couch petting the dogs until I had to pee.

My urine was deep yellow; my life needs to change.

February 16th

Slept maybe two hours last night. I kept opening my eyes to look over at Joe's side of the bed.

Read your comment, DrFudge; thank you.

Do you ever sleep?

You seem like someone who would have troubles that keep them awake.

That is just a guess on my part.

There are no more secrets between Joe and I and it will take some time for all this ugliness to become beautiful---I want to believe it can. I have to believe what Joe and I are dealing with will lead to something good.

At work: Going through the motions, taking notes for this blog. Saw Yolanda in the parking lot with a cigarette, didn't know she smoked. People are still talking about what happened in the ladies' room. I eavesdropped while looking at my horse picture.

Anything is possible now at the end of the world.

At lunch I went out to get my Carl's Catch and fries. Unwrapping the paper with the bag on my lap revealed just the right amount of sauce. A few people looked my way as I carried my bag in; they probably smelled my fries.

Soon everything beautiful will be yours.

Someone had written that on the overtime board in yellow chalk.

Took more notes for this blog and looked at my pictures as I ate.

The horse looks so calm, so proud, like he knows that he is on his way to somewhere good.

A couple of minutes ago Yolanda leaned into my cubicle.

She looked calmer than I've seen her in weeks and I didn't smell sweat.

"Could I see you in my office?" She asked.

I smiled and told her I'd wrap my food up and be right in.

Two gals were taking a selfie in the cubicle across the way.

They were both laughing as the one with the phone worked to get the light and angle right. The phone flashed as it captured two happy women---

As it captured what had been mistaken for a chew toy.

As it captured a moment of pure expression in a bathroom.

After she got the shot, they passed the phone back and forth and looked happy.

"It's perfect!" One of the gals said.

Perfect---imagine that.

And now I'm off to see what Yolanda wants.

Maybe she needs more help with the bathroom--

Maybe she found something that confused her in a desk drawer.

We'll see.

The

das glas das glas das glas das glas das glas das glas das glas das glas

Glads das glas das glas das glas das glas das glas das glas das

glas das glas das glas das glas das glas das glas das glas das glas das
glas das glas das glas das glas das glas das glas das glas das glas das

(Jim Belushiglas das glas das glas das glas das glas

das glas das glas das **in Purgatory)** glas das glas das

glas das glas das glas das glas das glas das glas das glas das glas das
glas das glas das glas das glas das glas das glas das glas das glas das
glas das glas das glas das glas das glas das glas das glas das glas das
glas das glas das glas das glas das glas das glas das glas

I have no idea why I am here. Seriously—none.

There has to be a reason, though, right? I mean, things like this don't just happen--I had to have done *something*, right?

I just have no idea what that is.

After I moved here somebody painted, "Albanians fuck goats" above my door.

Yeah, great—my family is Albanian, ha ha ha.

I find myself looking up at the words every time I leave my apartment. Back in the real world people razzing Albanians was something I could laugh along with or at least shrug off. Not here: In this place it strikes a nerve. Maybe I'm sick of Them always messing with me; They fuck with you 24/7 here.

Every morning a Jeep Compass shows up to take me to the set of *The Glads.*

Every morning I can hear "A Little Respect" by Erasure through the tinted glass.

They *know* that I can't stand Erasure and especially hate "A Little Respect." There is no point in complaining, though, there's no use in yelling at the driver to turn that shit off.

There is no off switch or stereo for that matter:

The music just plays, that's the way this place is.

I am in that car for exactly three minutes and thirty seconds. The set of *The Glads* is in the back of a Gamestop that always smells like grape bubblegum. One second I'm edging past kids browsing the new video games and the next a man who looks like Steve Buscemi is handing me the pages for the first scene. The scripts are the worst shit you could ever imagine: Think of every stupid thing you've ever seen in a sitcom and we've probably done it on *The Glads*.

As I look over the pages Chipper Dunn walks up with a smile equally patronizing and insane.
"This is going to be our best episode yet, Jim! Wait til you read it!"
"Yeah, sure, Chipper. Great," I force a smile, playing along.
Last time I *didn't* play along I had these nightmares about being on fire for a week. I could feel everything including my organs cooking and my skin blistering. Lesson learned. Now I smile and hold the script up as if to acknowledge reading them is something I have been waiting my whole life to do. Maybe I have. Maybe my life has been leading up to having a boss like Chipper Dung and living in a mall and starring in an awful sitcom.

I remember when all this started: I was walking in a mall, the experience seemed real but then I saw weird stuff and thought I was dreaming. Oh well, just a mall, right? There are far worse settings for a dream. *I'll wake up eventually.* This guy in a suit with a big smile walked up to me and extended his hand.

"I'm Chipper Dunn, Jim, pleasure to finally meet you."

I took the hand and shook it: People know me from *According to Jim* and the movies and The Blues Brothers. I have always tried to be cool with the fans as long as they are respectful.

"Nice to meet ya, Chipper."

His eyes locked on mine. Chipper's eyes are blue like sapphires with flecks of red that seem to pulse. I started to acknowledge who he probably is but knew if I did the dream would become a nightmare—

"You're not dreaming, Jim: You're dead."

OK, now bad shit happens like spooky music and Chipper's mouth unhinging to bite my head off as demons emerge from Baby Gap.

No, that would have been preferable because that is what happens in nightmares. Nightmares end. They're bad, but they end after a few minutes. This hasn't ended and I have the feeling it never will. Sometimes I hold onto the idea that maybe this *is* a dream. Maybe I am in a coma and the concept of time is fucked up. A coma would be a good alternative to this.

Chad plays my son on *The Glads* and is a bland sort of handsome. He likes to have sex with dogs and is fucking a golden retriever behind the set as I flip through the pages.

The dog looks confused, maybe it read the script.

Part of me thinks that I need to try and have a serious talk with Chad.

Part of me understands that Chad is dealing with this situation the best he can.

If he actually exists: There is always the possibility that Chad is a figment of my imagination or whatever this is.

In today's episode Chad takes the family car—(a lavender Jeep Compass)—out without asking. He gets a dent on it and struggles to keep me from finding out. There are laughs, some physical comedy bits, and in the end we all learn something...

It's enough to make you want to vomit in a boot.

We finish the last scene and the set grows silent as the lighting changes. The four Glads move to the middle of the set and begin waiting in a pool of light surrounded by darkness. The only sound is Chad chewing on his lips. What seems like ten minutes pass as I feel everything inside me tightening. The four of us call this time The Silent Scream, when we are waiting to see if Chipper is okay with the scenes or not. If not...

One time World War One soldiers rushed the stage with bayonets on the end of their rifles. They fired some shots and I felt a bullet rip through my right arm and another hit my groin. The soldiers charged into the pool of light and ran us through. I felt a bayonet pierce my skull and then---

We were reshooting as if nothing had happened.

The Silent Scream---this is why it is so important to give this deathless shit everything you have: When you don't Chipper has his ways of expressing his displeasure.

Today, though, he walked into the pool of light with a big smile.

"Great job, team! You guys rock!" He said brightly.

"Is it a wrap, Chipper?"

"Is it a wrap?!" Chipper laughed and then focused on me. He sent three quick but painful taps to the center of my brain before turning towards the crew somewhere out in the darkness. "I love this guy! Ladies and gentlemen, Jim Belushi!"

He turned back to me and the smile had grown dim and tighter.

"You loved your brother, didn't you, Jim?"

Fucking bastard.

"I *love* him, Chipper, not past tense," I said that firmly but carefully.

"Do you ever wonder what happened to him, Jim? You grew up with religion, right?"

"We went to the Albanian Orthodox Church but I don't know if you'd call us religious."

"But that church believes in heaven and hell, right?"

"Yeah, of course."

"Where do you think John went?"

I am not going to have an emotional reaction. No, this fucker doesn't get that. No way, man.; I am going to stay totally cool; I am in control.

"I have no doubt, Chipper; John had his problems but he was a good man."

I was biting back the tears---it doesn't matter how many years pass, this shit still gets to me and Chipper Dung knows this.

Chipper took a step closer to me. His smile was private and surprisingly warm. Even though I could see the rest of the cast out of the corner of my eye I got this weird feeling that Chipper and I are the only two people in whatever this place is and that is the way it has always been.

"Jim, you love your brother and, like you said, he was a good man. John was a very talented man who cast a big shadow," A tight, patronizing smile. "He only hurt himself, right? It wasn't like he was a murderer or a pedophile."

"He definitely was neither."

Chipper nodded and turned from me a little to look out into the darker edges of the set.

"But he was given a big talent, though, what some would call a *God given* talent..."

He trailed off before turning back to me with that horrible smug little grin of his.

I know where he's going with this and he knows that I know.

He also knows that I worry about this a lot, that John is somewhere nearby, down in this place. I keep dreading the day Chipper has him make a special guest appearance on *The Glads* because right now it is just a thought. It is, most likely, Chipper messing with my head. I believe that John is *somewhere else*---most of the time.

163

"Well, I'd love to talk, bro," Chipper's voice brings me back to the present. "But we've got to let all these well paid people get home! It's a wrap, folks, see you tomorrow."

I wave off the lime green Jeep Compass waiting to drive me home; I need to walk and lose myself in the crowd. This mall is like any other mall: Teens socializing, people carrying bags from the Gap, old people getting their exercise. Shortly after I got here I tried confronting shoppers by asking them if they knew where we were. I had been vaping, it was stupid. The people I was yelling at looked confused. Logical reaction, right? Security in the form of a bland looking guy in a blue mall cop outfit hustled over. He was White, not skinny, not fat, somewhere around 40---Diligent Dan.
"Excuse me, sir, I need you to curb your behavior," he said.
"Fuck you! You're a figment of my imagination rent-a-cop!"
A flash of blue...his arm? Heaviness. Something like a rock in my guts, wetness---
I looked down and saw that Diligent Dan had slashed my belly open and my intestines were falling out. Reflexively, I grabbed at them, trying to push them back in, my glistening pink intestines. They were slimy. I realized that I hadn't washed my hands and wondered if I would give myself sepsis. A moment after that thought the pain hit; it was like all the pain I had ever felt in my life had been rolled in a ball and shoved in my lap.

And then the moment ended: I was dead sober and standing in the middle of the mall fully intact with Diligent Dan standing in front of me.

Instead of a razor or whatever he had slashed me with he had a flyer.

"The bathrooms are back that way, sir," he smiled. "This flyer has a map of the mall to help you get around."

Not being a stupid guy I got the message: Don't fuck with Diligent Dan. Most times I run into him he gives me a friendly smile and nod. On rare occasions I do something I am not supposed to, however, he frowns and shakes his head slightly. Case in point: The exit doors. I fell in with the crowds moving towards the exit doors one time because I wanted to see what was outside the mall. Halfway to them I felt a hand on my arm.

Diligent Dan was right there, frowning and shaking his head.

I nodded and turned back the way I had come. I do not fuck with Diligent Dan or his clone army. All the mall security are Diligent Dans. Sometimes they walk in pairs of Diligent Dans having quiet Diligent Dan conversations.

Walking back from the shoot, I thought about Chipper needling me about John. Diligent Dan approached from the other direction. He gave me a smile and a nod and got both back from me. There are a lot of people in the mall at all times of the day. It's not Christmas crowd busy but there are a lot of people. Sometimes the crowds are comforting but sometimes—

Sometimes I wonder what they are: A figment of my imagination? Or, are they people like me who ended up here for whatever reason, spending an eternity walking between the GameStop and Hot Topic and Sbarro?

That shit can really mess with you if you let it.

My apartment is in the back of Toweltastic. a store that sells nothing but beach towels. I tried to interact with the people who work there in the beginning and it went something like this:

"Hey, how are you doing today? Manny, right? What do you do when you're not on the job, Manny?"

Blank stare. Big smile.

"What sort of towel are you looking for today, sir? We have many different kinds of towels to fill all your towel needs!"

Yeah, I don't bother talking to them anymore; I just walk to the back of the shop where the door to my apartment is.

Honey, I'm home! Cue laugh track.

No, that really happens: Every time I open the fucking door a recording of my voice yells "Honey I'm home!" which cues a laugh track. Every fucking time.

"My pan is full." An annoyed little voice from the couch.

"Hey, I missed you, too buddy."

Mr. Hate glowers at me from the red IKEA couch, his tail moving in quick angry twitches.

"If you're too busy to deal with it, Jim, I could do my business in other places."

"Okay okay, jeez, give a guy a second, okay?"

"I would do it myself but I don't have thumbs..."

"Can I hit the pen first, bro? A nice hit and then litter box, okay?"

"Whatever." He closes his eyes, I have ceased to exist.

The cat I call Mr. Hate came with the apartment. I remember the day Diligent Dan showed me the place. Mr. Hate came strolling out, tail up, watching me curiously. I walked over and crouched down to pet his back. He moved away and looked at me with pure contempt.

"Yeah, no, I'm not into you that way, Jim."

I leapt back. Yeah, I pissed my pants a little but THE CAT JUST TALKED!!

Mr. Hate looked up at me, studying my face.

"Are you just going to stand there like a big retard or are you going to clean my shit box?"

This is our relationship: I feed him and clean his litter box and he stares at me as if I am an intruder. Sometimes, he messes with my head.

How is this different from any other relationship I have had with cats in the past?

To say Mr. Hate fouls his litter box would be an understatement.
When I am done I go to the couch with the vape pen and wait for
the latest episode of *The Glads*. It doesn't matter that I am the star
of the show, it is *required* viewing.

If I walked out into Toweltastic the show would be playing, same
situation out in the mall; no one escapes *The Glads*, no one.

The theme song is so terrible Diane Warren would cut off one of
her own tits to escape it. The tune is played by the most
incompetent steel drum band in existence and sung by a drunk
sounding Alan Thicke impersonator---

In other words, it is the perfect theme music for our show.

We shoot an episode every day and they are aired maybe an hour
after Chipper calls a wrap. We film so fast and rehearse so little
that you can see us looking at the teleprompter.

We still manage to flub lines but I'm sure people enjoy that because
it means that much less of the script to endure.

It takes several deep hits to get through the episode. As the credits
roll Mr. Hate scowls at me from the far end of the couch.

"You know, watching you is like watching your brother." He pauses,
his tail moving in lazy arcs. "Without the talent, of course"

Nothing like a loving pal.

"Ain't you a sweetheart," my words ride a wave of smoke. "I spit in
your food, by the way."

"Don't worry I could taste it. Can we try a different brand? That kind tastes like an Albanian's underpants."

But he knows there is only one brand: The kibble and human food just *appears* in the kitchen.

Mr. Hate likes messing with me, that's all.

After the show I walk down the mall to the bar. The cherry pie strain put me in a good mood and I wave to the shoppers and a wary looking Diligent Dan clone. Are any of them the original Diligent Dan or are all of them clones? If they are all clones, where is the original?

This is the sort of thinking that can drive you mad in a place like this.

YepperDeppers is a rip off of Chili's or TGIFridays. I always sit with the other cast members at the same table every night. Have I ever asked if they are in Hell themselves or if they are simply figments of my own imagination? No, and probably for the same reason they never have asked me that: Odds are that it's better not to know. In one corner a man eats a huge bowl of chili.

Huge---human head sized. Considering where we are I wouldn't be surprised if that was entirely appropriate.

"Oh my God! This is the worst fucking chili ever!"

He shovels two more heaping spoonfuls into his mouth. His face is smeared to a degree it looks as if he is wearing a mask made out of chili.

"This chili tastes worse than my grandfather's asshole!"

Chili man eats another twenty seconds before making another comment about the awfulness of the chili.

He is in YepperDepper's every night and always orders the chili.

Chad is wearing a t-shirt with an abstract photo on the front; my guess would be that it's an extreme close up of a dog's asshole. Kelly, the 25 year old who plays my 15 year old daughter, has a bowling ball sized mound of coke in front of her. Her eyes are wide open and she has a cocaine mustache. Glory, the woman who plays my wife, is eating a huge cheeseburger with two pints of heavy looking beer in front of her. There is a stage across the restaurant where one of two bands plays between reruns of *The Glads*. One is kind of emo and is called Mope. All the members wear eyeliner and look sullen. The other is a metal band called Scowl that announces "This one is called Burnt Cheez-Whiz " between every song. Every night is like this. Every third night it is somebody's birthday and all the diners are supposed to sing the special YepperDeppers happy birthday song. If you don't, one of the Diligent Dans comes to your table with a subtle head shake and frown.

After a couple of hours I say goodnight and head out into the mall. What time is it? There are no windows, no natural light, and no clocks so it is impossible to tell. I vape or smoke until I fall asleep. I sleep without dreams. I wake up, eat breakfast, and then it is time to go to the set. Time is meaningless. I have no idea how long I have been here—weeks? Months? Years? Decades? Something else not to dwell on.

Someone is walking beside me; I smell his expensive cologne and know it is Chipper Dunn. I have the weird feeling that we are in the same part of the mall I found myself in when he told me that I was dead.

"Numbers are great, Jim. We've been renewed!"

He has told me this at least two times since I have been here. What does that mean? Two years?

"Excellent news, Chipper."

A little kid who is maybe seven or eight is talking animatedly to a man who is probably his father. It seems so normal, so innocent, that my emotions nearly overwhelm me.

"I can answer any questions you may have, Jim."

"I appreciate that Chipper, but I'm okay." It's probably better not knowing.

"Right-o chief! Go team!"

He turns around and walks back in the opposite direction whistling Erasure's Chains of Love. I look around for the kid and his father but they are gone. They seemed so real, so painfully tangible---I think about John and every breath has a weight to it. I walk through Toweltastic ignoring all the smiling faces asking me how they can fill my towel needs.

I walk into my apartment ignoring the resentful expression of my cat.

I climb into bed fully clothed and pull the covers over my head. Another day ends.

letzte chance auf der treppe letzte chance auf der treppeletzte chance auf der treppeletzte chance auf der treppeletzte chance auf der treppeletzte chance auf der treppeletzte chance

auf der treppeletzte chance auf der treppeletzte chance **Last** auf der treppeletzte

chance auf der treppeletzte chance auf der treppeletzte **Chance** Chance auf

der treppeletzte chance auf der treppeletzte chance auf der treppeletzte **On** chance auf

der treppeletzte chance auf der treppeletzte chance auf der treppeletzte **The** chance

auf der treppeletzte chance auf der treppeletzte chance auf der treppeletzte

Stairway chance auf der treppeletzte chance auf der treppeletzte chance

auf der treppeletzte chance auf der treppe

173

I had been staying in Room 314 of the Comfort Suites in Fernley, Nevada. Business travel, something to take care of in Reno thirty miles to the west. The morning this started, I packed up and left the suite. The hall looked the same as when I had walked down it the previous afternoon: Brown carpet in a herringbone pattern. Cream colored walls. A series of doors with numbers beginning in "3." There has to be some detail I missed but to be honest I wasn't paying attention; my life is hotel corridors and I tend to not see them anymore. The hall ended at a door to the stairs on the left and a lift. The down button was not lit so I pushed it. Nothing happened, no ding or sound of the elevator coming to life from below. A woman came out of one of the rooms: Asian, probably Filipina. Between 30 and 40. Small in stature but fit. Movements agile. Wearing an orange, two piece bikini---

That detail was a small, red light; there was no pool or spa in the hotel.

The woman looked confused; confused, angry, and a bit scared.

"What the fuck?" She asked the cream colored wall in front of her. Her other emotions were becoming more secondary to fear, I could see that and approached her; the stranger was scared but trying to push that emotion down---a fighter, a strong person.

"Where do you think you are?" I asked. The question just came up, I do not know why.

"I...was about to leave my cabana to go to the beach....sit and watch the waves."

"Try and get back into your room." Again, no idea why that suggestion came to me.

She looked confused but after a few seconds fished her room key out of the small purse she was carrying. The key didn't work. I walked down to 314, my key didn't work either.

Another woman was coming out a door further down the hall rubbing her hands: Black. Somewhere around 40. Nice business clothes. Decent shape but I could tell her reflexes were slow. She walked into the hall and looked confused just as the other woman had and I was feeling myself.

"Where did you come from?" The Filapena asked.

"What do you mean?" The black woman asked. "The bathroom, this---"

"Isn't where you expected to be, same for us," I explained.

"325," the woman in the business suit said softly, noting the number on the door she had walked through.

"What's going on?" She looked to the Filipina and myself to answer that.

"No fucking idea," the woman in the bikini said loudly. "But someone is gonna hear about it."

"Hear about it?" The woman in the suit asked.

"Fuck yeah. This cabana cost three hundred a night, I paid extra to be on the beach...this is not the beach!"

"A refund is probably the least of your concerns," I pointed out.

"You work for the hotel?" Bikini asked me harshly.

"No…"

"Lucky for you."

"Do your cell phones work?" Business suit asked. "I left mine at my desk."

I pulled mine out of my pocket, there was no signal. Bikini didn't have hers.

"Look, this is weird," Business suit said, it was clear she was struggling to remain calm. "But there has to be an explanation, someone who can help us."

I nodded but did not feel as optimistic. I had been in fucked up situations before and this had the same vibe, a certain *things are fucked* vibe. We walked down to the lift. Bikini jammed her right index finger on the down button repeatedly but nothing happened.

"Looks like we'll have to take the stairs," I pointed out.

A door crashed open next to 314 and a man stepped out in a hurry: White. Around 50. Reddish receded hair and matching goatee. Most importantly, an M-16 was in his hands. My suitcase was locked, there was nothing to do but move in on him unarmed. It was clear he did not have military training, the way he stood and held the gun

175

gave me that impression. I took the gun away and backed up a couple of steps with it against my chest. The three other people in the hall looked scared for at least two different reasons.

"What the hell?" Goatee said, reaching for his rifle but then drawing his hands back.

"Why are you carrying a gun?" I demanded.

Something blended with his fear and confusion---cunning.

"It's my second amendment right to bear arms," and then he looked around at the hall. "This is not the parking garage."

He looked over at Bikini Woman and clearly liked what he saw: Even in fucked up times men will be men.

"We all came from different places," I explained.

"Where are we?" Goatee asked.

"This looks like the hallway outside my suite, but it probably isn't," I said

"We need to go down the stairs," Business Suit said firmly. "Find someone who can tell us what is going on."

No one voiced opposition to that, the four of us walked out the door to the stairway. I had a moment of concern about leaving my suitcase there but a moment later realized there would be no one to mess with it.

We were on a cement landing two meters by one. This was the top floor.

"302," Bikini said, looking at the number on the metal door. "It can't be 302 floors, no buildings are that high.

"It must mean something else," Business suit said.

I took the flashlight from my pocket and leaned over the rail, there was an Escher like series of switchbacks leading down forever.

Yeah, 302 and floors seemed possible...even if it didn't.

"What do you see?" Goatee asked.

"We're more than three floors up. There's nothing for us to do but start heading down."

Bikini tried the knob to the door marked 302, it was no longer turning.

176

"This makes no damn sense," Goatee said. He was trying to sound gruff but I could pick up on the fear in his voice.

We walked down one flight then two and eventually ten.
"Damn," Goatee said.
"What?" Business suit asked.
"I've gotta piss."
"Go up a couple of floors, we'll wait for you here," I said.
He looked at me and then started up the stairs. We heard his heavy steps echoing on the heavy treads. The footsteps stopped. A few moments later something was dripping on the landing in front of me.
"Go in the corner, please!" I shouted up.
"Sorry!" He yelled back, more than a little sarcasm in his tone.
A minute passed then two. He *had* to have been done.
"You nearly finished?"
No response, and we hadn't heard his boots on the treads.
"We can send someone up to find him," Bikini said.
"I don't think so," I said. "Let's give it a few minutes."
After two minutes I walked up one flight, making sure I could see Bikini and Business Suit; my instincts were telling me not to let them out of my sight.
Another minute passed and then I heard Goatee's footsteps but they were coming from *below*. Sure enough, he appeared on the landing with the others; all three of them appeared as confused as I felt.
"What the hell?" Goatee's voice was a whisper. "I was heading *down* the stairs."
"Why did you make me leave my gun?" He looked up at me accusingly. "We're in a big ol' mess."
"Do you really think a gun is going to help here?" I asked.
He just shook his head and looked at the stairs he had just come up.

"We need to stay in sight of each other at all times," Business suit said as we walked down one flight then three then eight.
"Ah, fuck!" Bikini said.
"What?"
She pointed at the fire door she was standing next to, it said "415."

Now I was getting rattled despite all my training and everything else.

Be calm. That can't stand for floors, it has to mean something else.
I told myself that but there was the matter of Goatee going up the stairs when he had been certain he had been going down.
"All we can do is keep heading down," I said as calmly as possible. "These stairs have to end somewhere."

"We need to stop, bro, I'm gettin' a charley horse," Goatee, stopping on a landing to massage his right calf. He looked up at me with curiosity.
"The way you came at me and took my gun, you in the Army or something?"
"That's irrelevant," I said, maybe a little too firmly.
"Whatever, bro," he snorted.
"Now I've gotta pee," Bikini whined.
"We shouldn't get out of sight of one another," Business suit said firmly.
"I'm not going in front of him," Bikini shrugged towards Goatee.
"We'll stay in sight, one flight apart. You," I gestured towards Business Suit.
"Janelle," she said.
"Yes, Janelle can keep an eye on you, I can keep an eye on her and--"
"Roy," Goatee said.
"Roy can keep an eye on me."
The four of us fanned out. After a few moments, Roy cried out in disgust.
"Hey, stick to the corner!" He yelled.
"Sorry," Bikini called from a couple of floors above.
"Get done quick," Janelle said.
"Why?" Bikini asked, her voice sounded odd, further away.
"Just do it!"
Janelle and I were a flight apart, fourteen steps...no twenty. Wait---

And then the two women came running down together and all three of us hurried down to Roy who was trying to act like a tough guy with limited success.

"You were getting real far away," he said softly.

"I know," was my response.

Every few landings one of us would knock on a fire door as we tried the latch---there was no response.

"I'll be damned," Roy said, starting to head down the next flight.

"What?" Bikini asked.

"Come check it out."

We did, there was a case of bottled water.

I didn't like that; someone knew we'd be coming down the stairs and had left that for us, my instincts told me that. Would it be poisoned? No, that would end their fun. Roy got to the case and looked up at me as did Bikini and Janelle.

"I'm guessing it's fine," I said. "As fine as anything can be in this situation."

"Someone is playin' a game," Roy nodded grimly after taking a drink.

"You think?" Janelle sounded unsure. "How could someone be doing this? She--"

"Doreen," Bikini said.

"Doreen was in a cabana in Mexico," Janelle continued. "I was in the bathroom in my office building in Boise. Roy was---"

We all looked at the man with the goatee, he looked very uncomfortable.

"It doesn't matter," I said. "We're here now."

"What about you?" Doreen looked at me suspiciously.

"What about me? I was in a hotel in Fernley, Nevada on business."

"Must be good business," the woman in the bikini said with a canny smirk. "That's a five thousand dollar suitcase."

"Whatever," Roy said softly. "It don't matter now, all that matters is getting out of here."

We had walked past sixty fire doors and everyone's legs were sore. The four of us paused on a landing and stopped.

"This concrete is awful on my skinny ass," Doreen said.

"You don't need to worry about that. "

Janelle said in a tone of voice that made it sound like she was under hypnosis. She was looking down at the next landing. I walked over to see what she saw: A pile of eight pillows, neatly stacked, and four blankets neatly folded. I looked around for cameras out of habit---if there were cameras they were very cleverly hidden.

"How many floors have we gone down?" Doreen asked, her voice was unusually calm.

"I've counted sixty doors so….sixty," I replied.

"Even old skyscrapers like the Empire State are over a hundred floors," Roy pointed out.

Very true, but it didn't explain how we had all seen the others get further away. Had we been drugged somehow? Something through the vents in my hotel? The others could be actors, I had worked with people who definitely had the means to set something like that up----No, I was sober and looking at the others I could see they were, as well.

This was something different, something I had never experienced.

"Let's say the tallest building in the world is 250 floors," Roy suggested. "If we go down...what, 190? We go down 190 more floors then that has to be the bottom."

We were all sitting on pillows with blankets wrapped around us. There was probably food waiting a few more floors down.

"We should rest some before continuing," Janelle said. She looked scared, on the verge of some sort of anxiety attack, but was working to stay calm.

"Nothing is going to hurt us," I said. "I have the feeling if they wanted to, it would have happened by now."

"You sure know a lot," Roy barked, starting to stand up. "Maybe this is some government shit, some sort of psy ops, and you're the inside person."

He looked as if he were about to come at me. I wasn't concerned about that action but feared how an altercation would affect morale.

"Even if that's the truth," Janelle said, "we're not just getting out because you're onto whatever is going on. Sit back down. Relax."
He did, reluctantly.

"So...you were walkin' out of your room, Doreen out of a cabana, Janelle out of a bathroom, and I was walking into a parking garage---but we all ended in the hallway of your hotel."

Roy was trying to reason through things but clearly the fact we had met in *my* hallway continued to make him suspicious of me.

We passed the seventieth fire door then the seventy-fifth and then the eightieth.

"What if we aren't actually going down," Janelle said at one point.

"What do you mean?" I asked.

"Early on, after Roy went to the bathroom and we lost him he was *certain* that he had been heading down the stairs."

"I was, I am," he nodded.

"Fucking great," Doreen muttered.

"We should just keep heading down and hope for the best," Janelle sighed.

There was a silver platter on the landing of the eighty-third floor---real silver, Doreen confirmed it with a nod of appreciation.
"Nice, probably cost a couple hundred," she said.

There were a dozen energy bars on it, normal brands, nothing out of the ordinary---

Except everything was out of the ordinary in that place. Doreen shoved a couple of the bars in her little purse, wearing a blanket like a poncho. As three of us grabbed food off the tray, Janelle looked up the flight of stairs we had just come down.

"What if we only *think* we're going down?" She mused softly.

"I feel it," Roy replied harshly. "I feel myself bein' pulled down by gravity, I feel it in the *front* of my legs; we're goin' down."

"I---" Doreen started.

She didn't finish her thought---the lights went out.

"Join hands!" I yelled.

We did, I felt one of Roy's rough hands and Doreen's tiny ones.

"Someone get Janelle?" I asked.

"Yeah," Doreen said.

"What the fuck is going on?" Roy, thoughtful, a little shaky. Somewhere below us, there was the sound of some metal being tapped on a metal railing: Clank. Clankclank. Clank. Pause. Clank. Clankclankclank. Clank.

"Hey!" Roy yelled. "Where are we? How do we get out?"

"They're just messing with us," Janelle said.

The lights came back on. Doreen gasped---the silver tray was gone. Roy started running down the stairs as fast as he could manage; the rest of us pursued him, concerned about what would happen if we got separated. After one flight, he slipped and almost fell but caught himself with the rail and slammed into the wall. Roy sank to the nearest tread and sat there wheezing.

"They were already gone," Janelle said. "You weren't going to catch them."

What troubled me was that the silver tray was gone. Roy had been almost *standing* on it---how had we not felt someone come up? How had *I* not felt someone? The only answer was that no one had been there---

The only answer didn't make any sense.

We reached the 100th floor. Roy and Janelle were staggering, you could see their legs trembling.

"We need to stop," I said.

"I wanna get to the bottom of this," Roy replied as Doreen pounded on the door and shook the latch to no avail.

The man with the goatee watched her rattling the latch, something was clearly on his mind.

"You look like you want to say something," Janelle said to him.

"I don't know...I'm just keyed up---"

"Did something happen before you ran into the parking garage?" I asked.

Roy looked at me sharply but he was too scared or weirded out or *something* to be angry.

"I was at a protest. Me and a couple of my buddies showed up...maybe it was stupid but we thought we could stop some of the riotin'."

"Which is why you had the gun," Janelle said.

"Yeah. The thing is...one of the antifa people, he pulled out a handgun, a 9mm piece. A buddy and me, we froze; we couldn't shoot the dude even if he was aiming a piece at us. Mike, though...he was fixin' to turn his M4 on that liberal piece of shit but the antifa bro was quick, got Mike in the upper chest...must have been his heart cause he just dropped. Bill and I ran, just started running for the parking garage. There were pops behind us, the antifa dude shooting, but I guess we got lucky."

"Maybe you got killed and this is hell," Doreen said nonchalantly. We all looked at her, that seemed the last thing any of us should have been voicing out loud.

"This is not hell," Janelle said firmly. "Something is going on, but we're not dead."

"You sure of that?" Roy asked. "You remember exactly what happened in the bathroom?"

He looked over at me.

"What about you? I take you for a hired killer; maybe a rival got the drop on you in your hotel room."

"Got the drop on me? This isn't the movies."

"Kinda feels like one," Janelle sighed.

"*Do* you remember what happened in the bathroom?" Doreen asked Janelle.

The black woman raised her eyebrows at the younger woman.

"What do people usually do in the bathroom?"

She said that wryly but it was clear to me that Janelle was troubled by something. I looked at her, she met my gaze, shook her head, and started down the next flight of stairs.

At the 106th floor things changed, everything became orange, the stairs, walls and railings. The walls and treads were no longer cement; the former was painted sheetrock and the latter carpeted.

The railings were wood that had, somehow, been stained orange. Even the lighting had an orange hue.

"I don't like this," Janelle said softly.

She looked up the stairs and as she did the flights behind us went dark; the only light was coming from further down the stairs. Music was coming from somewhere down below, where we were heading---really old rock and roll.

"Rock Around the Clock," D said. "My husband used to listen to all that old rock music from the 50s."

She had been rubbing her stomach for awhile. It seemed to be unconscious which made me even more curious so I asked about it.

"I had stomach problems in the cabana---"

"Montezuma's Revenge," Roy nodded.

"What?" Doreen looked at him as if he had said something weird.

"The shits," Roy explained.

"Gross, but...yeah. I was going to the beach because it was the first time in a couple of days I felt good enough to leave the cabana. My stomach was still bad, but I felt I could at least be on the beach for fifteen minutes or so."

"You seemed okay when you walked into the hallway," I pointed out.

"I was scared, maybe it distracted me from how I physically felt."

Below us the song changed. It was one even I recognized: Johnny B Goode by Chuck Berry but the recording had things added, conga drums and flashes of dissonant strings. All of us paused on the next landing. No one rattled the latch of the (orange) door or knocked. We just stood on the landing, unable to look at each other, unable to walk on. The lights went on the flight we had just descended and began to flicker on the landing we were on. Chuck Berry was still singing, but his voice sounded more hysterical, wilder, but it was still Chuck Berry. Feedback flashed into the song as a counterpoint to the strings and the rhythm grew more primitive.

"What the fuck is going on," Janelle whispered.

I looked over at her; that had been the first time we heard her swear.

We continued descending: 107th floor, 108th, 109th. The fire doors no longer had numbers but black ink drawings: A snow capped mountain. A child going down a slide.

"This is bullshit," Doreen said, stopping in her tracks.

All of us stopped and looked over at her.

"We are playing along," the woman with the poncho continued. "They want us to go do so we have been going down---what if we went up?"

"There's nothin' up there but darkness," Roy said.

"Maybe, but she has a point," Janelle countered. "What happens if we don't play along."

"I don't see what we have to lose," I shrugged.

Roy almost said something then shook his head.

"Whatever, into the darkness...whatever," he grumbled.

We started up the stairs. The lights did not come on.

"We should join hands," Doreen said, we complied.

We should have been climbing away from the music but it got clearer: Chuck was now just shrieking and laughing and the guitars no longer bothered with the riff, playing wild notes and wails of feedback. One flight, Doreen leading us tread by tread. I expected them to end and D plummet into an abyss. That didn't happen...what happened was worse.

A second flight. It was so dark my eyes were no adjusting and---

Wait. I knew that sound, it was very faint but I could pick it up; I had trained myself to pick that variety of sound up.

Breathing. Something was breathing up ahead. I felt Doreen stiffen a couple of feet in front of me, clearly she heard it as well---or sensed it.

Something was in the dark with us...and then it was growling, the sound a big cat makes when you get too close.

"Doreen?" Janelle said behind me.

"Why would they kill us?" Doreen said shakily. "It would end their fun."

Would it? I have no idea why I thought that.

"That sounds like a mountain lion," Roy said, "we should turn back."

"It's not real," Doreen said. "I don't---"
And something was on her, knocking her back into me. Doreen
screamed, not just fear but pain and then she was just limp and
breathing raggedly in my arms. I struggled with her weight, Janelle
helped me and eventually Roy grabbed D's legs and the four of us
returned down the stairs and into the light.

Whatever it was had clawed Doreen's belly. The cuts were deep but
not fatal.
"There's a lot of blood," Janelle said weakly.
"Not as much as there could have been," I replied. "Anyone still
have water?"
"You won't need it," Roy sounded like he was half asleep.
I moved over to see what he was seeing; three steps down from the
landing we were on was a first aid kit.

I cleaned Doreen's wounds and bandaged them. The creature had
been huge, the way it had knocked Doreen and in turn me
backwards---it could have ripped her open...this was just a warning.
"Some warning," Doreen said, the cuts were deep enough to ache
and the way she winced the antiseptic clearly stung.
"You guys shoulda listened to me," Roy said quietly.
"Fuck that," Doreen turned on him. "You want to just play their
game?"
"Not playin' it almost got you killed," the man with the goatee
countered."Look, we got ninety floors left and then we'll be at the
bottom of the stairs."
"You're basing that on the logical assumption this building can't be
more than two hundred floors," Janelle said. "Logic....when Doreen
was just attacked by a jungle cat in the middle of a sealed stairwell.
We *came* from up there, if someone let that thing in we'd hear a fire
door opening and closing."
"They could do it real quiet and say thirty or forty floors up, then we
wouldn't hear it," Roy argued.
I held my hands up, the arguers looked over at me.

"I think next time we try something like that it will be far worse, let's just keep working our way down and try and figure out alternatives."

The Chuck Berry song abruptly ended, replaced by what Doreen identified as Buddy Holly, an undoctored Buddy Holly song. As the dead rock star sang about a girl named Peggy Sue, the four of us continued down the stairs.

117 floors then 120 and then 122.

Janelle cried out in pain and sat on a tread massaging her calf. All of our legs were in misery.

"We need a break if that's okay with you!" Doreen called out sarcastically.

The four of us sat down. Buddy Holly was replaced by two guys singing that all they had to do was dream.

"Everly Brothers," Doreen said. "But there's a lower voice in there---"

"Nick Cave," I said. "I know my post-punk."

"The drums are wrong," D frowned. "This sounds more like---"

"The guy who played drums for Al Green," Roy said.

All of us looked over at him.

"What?" The man with the goatee asked. "Can't a redneck like soul music?"

Doreen stood up and looked at the ceiling.

"Are we going to get a clue?" She asked loudly. "Are you going to let us know what you want from us?"

There was no response.

The carpet on the treads and the landings became a deeper pile, almost a shag. At the 125th floor landing there was an old photograph of a man with a pale moon face smiling at the camera.

"Fatty Arbuckle," Doreen said.

"Fatty *who*?" Janelle asked.

Doreen didn't respond, she was studying the photograph.

"He was a comedian in like the 1910s or something," she continued. "But he raped someone or something like that."

187

The man in the photo was no longer smiling, he was scowling and looking right at Doreen. His mouth was moving, I could make out the words:

I. Am. INNOCENT.

"Fuck this, just...fuck this," Roy raised his hands and started walking down the stairs. We fell in step behind him.

"What was that 120?" The man with the goatee said, taking the steps two at a time.

"125," I replied.

"Right," Roy continued. "We're doing a floor about every minute so in an hour and a half we should be at the bottom."

He sounded so rattled none of us cared to argue.

We were trapped in a stairwell with mountain lions and photographs that came to life.

"It could have been a screen," Janelle reasoned. "They've been using old footage of dead actors in commercials for a long time."

I looked at Roy and Doreen and could see they weren't buying J's logic. Looking at Janelle, I could see that she was just grasping at *any* explanation.

"Someone broke into my stall," she said. "A man."

"What happened?" Doreen asked.

"I don't know, I must have fought him off or something...he was breaking in and then I was at the sink washing my hands."

"Do you think you could have been raped and blacked out during it?" I had to ask.

A long pause, so long I didn't think she would reply.

"I don't know," Janelle said softly.

Roy had been shot at, Janelle had been assaulted in a bathroom, Doreen had suffered a serious case of the shits---

Had we died? No, all of us had dug our nails into skin until we bled; Doreen had bled quite a bit during the attack. From my experience I can say that dead people do not bleed. We passed the 130th floor. On the landing was a silver tray with sandwiches on it.

Roy grabbed one and started eating it. After a couple of large bites, he nodded to us.

"It's good, real good."

We were all hungry and spent a few minutes eating. My sandwich was exactly how I like it, the right amount of condiments, my favorite meat and cheese; it was as delicious as it was disconcerting. When I asked the others, they confirmed that their sandwiches were *perfect*.

Below the 132nd floor the stairwell grew narrower, three feet wide instead of four. The walls were no longer painted sheetrock, they were (orange) tuck and roll vinyl. Below the 134th floor the ceiling went from eight feet and lost a foot every floor we descended. Additionally, the stair width went from three feet to two. By the 138th floor we were crouching single file.

"This is ridiculous," Roy said. "Are we gonna have to go down the stairs on our knees?"

"No," Janelle said, stopping in front of him. "This is the end."

"What?" Doreen asked. "Is it a door?"

"No," J replied. "It's a wall, the same vinyl that's on the side walls, padded."

"They've left us no choice," Doreen said loudly. "We have to go back."

She was at the back of the line and turned to go up the stairs. D got a couple of feet before stopping.

"There's a wall back here, too," she sounded and looked confused.

"What are we supposed to do?" Roy asked.

All of us sat on treads. There was such little space, each of us had our knees in the back of the person in front of us. The walls seemed to be pulsing, like we were inside a living thing, smelled like it, too---meat and blood and sweat. The heat rose and our little tomb was immediately stifling.

"We're gonna suffocate!" Doreen moaned.

That was a distinct possibility.

"Look," I said, it took effort as we were already getting short on air. "They are probably just messing with us; what fun are we to them if we're dead?"

"This wall feels weird," Doreen said. "It's wet."

"Wet?" Janelle asked.

The words were barely out of her mouth when hole big enough for a man to stick his head through opened in the wall D had been talking about and water gushed through the hole.

"Ah, come on, man!" Roy protested.

Janelle was getting the worst of it being at the bottom. I saw Roy struggling to pull her back. I writhed around so I could help him and Doreen was trying to grab me---we were all fucked, the water was coming in too fast and there was no place to go. The force of the stream was powerful enough to push Doreen into the three of us.

"Something's pulling at my feet!" Janelle sputtered.

"A hand?" Roy asked.

"No, like suction. Hold on to my arm, I'm going to feel with my feet...there's an opening."

J looked back at us with determination.

"Let me go, I'm going to try and get through," She said.

We did, she eased into the hole and then disappeared. The hole had slowed our crypt from filling up but more water was coming in than going out.

"Shit, I may as well try," Roy said.

He eased down into the hole. Bigger than Janelle, he got stuck which presented a problem for himself and also one for Doreen and I---R was now blocking the outflow from our prison. The hole behind Doreen was now big enough that she could have squeezed through it if the pressure weren't so great and the space we were in wasn't nearly full of water. I took a deep breath and pushed Roy's shoulders with my feet and used my hands on the treads for leverage; he was beginning to move. Doreen was gasping in an air pocket, panicking, I grabbed her ankle and when she looked down at me I motioned for her to follow. The crypt area was now full of water. Roy was moving, it felt like too little too late---

And then I was moving down a short tunnel so narrow I'm surprised Roy got through at all. Touching the sides, they felt like wet skin---and then I was out with Doreen right behind me. There was a gush of water as she was released then no more. We were on a landing, normal sized, quickly drying. The next flight of stairs also appeared normal. Looking behind, those stairs looked normal as well.

It was getting to be a struggle to keep my shit together....

You've trained for situations like this, just take a breath; calmness is your natural state. Calmness...

"No, I think I'm gonna lose my shit."

Had I said that out loud? Yep; everyone was looking at me.

"Ignore me," I sighed. "It's been a long day."

The four of us were still wet but our surroundings were dry---we had been trapped in a living womb that had disappeared, all the water had immediately dried, pictures were coming to life...nope, nothing to see here.

"This isn't a dream," I continued. "We feel pain, we bleed, so we must be awake and alive."

"Buck up," Roy said softly. "Only sixty-one floors to go."

I nodded even if I wasn't so sure.

We passed the 140th floor and then the 142nd and the 145th.

"Oh my God," Doreen said.

I looked over; she had opened the fire door. We all rushed over and through the door without thinking, even me.

I should have known it wouldn't be that easy.

"Where are we?" D asked loudly.

We were out on a field, but it looked like a battle had taken place there complete with blackened craters and barbed wire and smoke in the air.

"We need to go back through the door," I said.

"What?" Roy asked.

"I think---"

And then there was yelling and men were climbing out of trenches a couple hundred yards to our left. They were in World War One

191

uniforms, British Army, and they were charged towards us with fixed bayonets. To our right, the Germans were going over a top and making a similar charge. I looked behind us, the door was gone.

Of course it was.

Shots were whistling all around us.

"This cannot be real," Janelle said, I could tell by her voice she was going into shock.

"Run!" Doreen yelled.

I was hit numerous times; it felt like someone flicking me hard but I knew it was a bullet hitting me. It didn't kill me, didn't even slow me down. We were running towards where the door had been. A shell whistled and exploded next to Doreen. I saw her arm blown off in a spout of blood and pieces of flesh but she kept running---

And then we were back on the landing. The others were checking themselves, I assumed they had felt the "flicks" as well. Doreen's left arm was whole again, skinny and brown as it had been before.

"Maybe we should look before goin' through another door," Roy said.

None of us responded.

We continued down the stairs, passing the 150th floor, then the 154th and 157th. There was a new sound, heels clicking on a hard material a couple of floors above us; how heels could be clicking on carpet...well, there was no logic to that place.

"Someone is behind us," Doreen said loudly.

She stopped as if planning to wait for the stranger to catch up.

And then the stranger laughed, a very cold, cruel sounding laugh.

It's Jack the Ripper...he never died because he was never alive, not really, just a spirit, a vengeful one...

I do not know when I thought that; I was not about to freak out the others---

"It's a vampire, I know it." Doreen, on the other hand, had no such qualms.

"Vampires don't exist," Janelle said through a mouth of clenched teeth.

More heel clicks, more of the evil sounding laughter. The stranger was closer, two flights above I'd guess. Doreen cried out and started running down the stairs, almost knocking Janelle over who started running as well followed by Roy. I want to say I ran with them because I didn't want us to get separated, the professional in me would like to believe that---the truth, however, was different.
 The clicking stopped---
That's because Jack is flying, soaring after us...mouth unhinging, scalpel in hand...
Not helping, not helping at all.
Two flights down Doreen stopped and we almost collided with each other.
"It's gone," Janelle said before looking at Doreen. "You thought it was a vampire?"
"Yeah."
"After you said that, I imagined it was a vampire as well."
"Vampires don't exist," I said firmly.
"You imagined *somethin'*," Roy said triumphantly. "You looked scared, scared as I've ever seen anyone."
"What did you imagine?" Doreen demanded, stepping towards me. I just shook my head and walked on.

We passed the 195th floor, then the 197th, and 199th.
"Almost there!" Roy yelled. I could tell by his voice that he was smiling.
Doreen giggled and took the lead down the last step. On the last fire door was not an enigmatic picture but one of the most beautiful words in the English language: EXIT. D pushed open the door and looked out carefully.
"It's just a hall."
All four of us walked through a door a few seconds ago and at this moment I am the only one who knows where we are: It's obvious to me, maybe the others are blocking it out. We came through the door marked EXIT and across the hall is a door marked "315." I have no idea how they'll react when they realize we are back where we started. They may want to stay in this corridor but poison gas or

scorpions will force us through the door at the end of the hall and back into the stairwell.

And we will have no choice but to head down the stairs.

oma oma oma oma oma oma oma oma oma oma oma oma oma oma
oma oma oma oma oma oma oma oma oma oma oma oma oma oma
oma oma oma oma oma oma oma oma oma oma oma oma oma oma
oma oma oma oma oma oma oma oma oma oma oma oma oma oma
oma oma oma oma oma oma oma oma oma oma oma oma oma oma
oma oma oma oma oma oma oma oma oma oma oma oma oma oma
oma oma oma oma oma oma oma oma oma oma oma oma oma oma

oma oma oma oma oma oma oma oma **Grandma** oma
oma oma oma oma oma oma oma oma oma oma oma oma oma oma
oma oma oma oma oma oma oma oma oma oma oma oma oma oma
oma oma oma oma oma oma oma oma oma oma oma oma oma
        oma oma oma oma oma oma oma oma
oma oma oma oma oma oma

oma oma oma oma oma oma oma oma

Hey,

Just wanted to touch base, see how things have been with you.
Finals are coming up, right? How's that anthropology class going?
I know you were having a tough time with it last time we spoke on
the phone; I remember you telling me the professor's name, it was
a weird name, sounded Eastern European, way more consonants
than vowels. Grandma always gets a kick out of crazy names like
that—
She would love to see you, you know...
You never respond when I ask if you're planning to come and see
her.
She's part of your family, you know, she loves you. In fact, she asked
about you when I visited her yesterday.

Grandma has been pretty lucid recently; I always look forward to
her good days---for about a week she had been having terrible
hallucinations. She kept talking about her youngest child (William)
going down with the Titanic. It was frightening to see her so upset,
going on and on about how cold the water must have been and the
terror Billy must have felt. I told you about William, right? I don't
know why she thought he drowned with all of those people on the
Titanic; like I said, some days her dementia is worse than others. It

was so vivid to her, though: She really believed William died on that ship and I said nothing, just tried to comfort her. Would it have been better to remind her he was shot on one of the last days of the war? How he had climbed out of his trench to have a look and the Germans picked him off? According to the report he probably didn't feel anything when that sniper shot him in the head. Should I have reminded grandma about that? Would that have made her feel better? I'm not sure.

We need to move grandma soon which means filling out a lot of forms. It was my first time doing her paperwork and I was nervous; her documentation is getting more difficult because everything is computerized now but I found some people to help me for a reasonable price. You want to know something funny? Once I got past my nervousness it was kind of exciting—at first I was anxious about getting caught, but then it became kind of fun, like being the star of a spy movie or something. You know me, my life is pretty boring, I think you've told me that yourself: *Dad, your life is boring.* I guess it is. Without a doubt Grandma is the most exciting part of it.

Grandma is going by the name Betsy Rathblodt now; if you come to visit, you will need to refer to her by that name.
I hope you will come to visit, she would really love to see you.

I feel like a broken record every time I write to you or we speak on the phone and I ask when you are coming to visit her---you never respond.

When we spend time in person you get angry when the subject comes up---

Believe me, I understand: When I was your age I felt the same way. My life was a mess, I was struggling to figure out a career and all sorts of other things; the last thing I needed was looking after an elderly person. But then Dad had his heart attack and couldn't look after Grandma anymore---

I was really angry about it but what could I do?

From time to time I still resent the fact he had my Aunt Jill to help him with Grandma while I have been taking care of her on my own. I guess it would have been more fair to you if your mother and I had more children but the marriage fell apart before we could make that happen. Your mother never knew what to make of Grandma; maybe it was a mistake telling her the truth---I think your mother was actually scared of Grandma.

Imagine that: Scared of a frail old lady in a hospital bed who has trouble going to the bathroom by herself.

I know you have problems with Grandma, too; I remember you telling me a few years back of some bad dreams that took place in a cemetery, coming upon a headstone with three dates written on it. The thing is, Grandma would never hurt you, she loves you.

Even if she wanted to hurt you she couldn't: Grandma is very frail. Most days she just lies in bed but a couple of weeks ago she actually wanted to go for a walk around the hospital. We had a bit of a problem when this older woman recognized her and called out one of the old names Grandma used. It turns out that the lady had been one of Grandma's nurses back in the 1960s or maybe it was the 50s. This is one of the reasons we need to move Grandma; most likely the nurses just thought the former nurse was just a confused old woman calling Grandma a name that isn't on her paperwork but we can't risk it.

This reminds me of a story Aunt Jill told me about a mistake my father made. Grandma used to have this picture, she was much younger in it but you could still recognize that it was her. This was a battered black and white photo of her and William's son---her grandson---posing in front of this old car. In the picture, Billy Junior was wearing his army uniform because he was on leave from World War Two. Grandma must have been right around 80 then. She loved that old picture and insisted on having it on her nightstand. Dad knew it was a bad idea but wouldn't say no to her. A nurse took notice of the picture and told some other people who came by just to look at that old photograph. This was in the late 80s, right before you were born. They asked my Dad about the picture and he said it was from the 1960s. One doctor pointed out the old car, which I want to say was a 1935 Chevrolet. Dad tried to play it off that our family was poor and drove old cars but another doctor noticed Billy's uniform was from World War Two---

Needless to say, they had to move her from the hospital shortly after that and get Grandma a new name.

I don't know what they'd do to her, I don't think anything bad, but you never know.

They'd definitely run tests, draw blood and study it.

Grandpa Billy was worried the government would take her somewhere; he was paranoid they'd run a bunch of awful tests on Grandma.

I don't know if that would happen but I won't risk anyone hurting her.

I have always been very careful; they would have to do a thorough search of our house to find anything incriminating. You remember when I scolded you for playing with that old chest? That was your great-grandfather's foot locker. We keep Grandma's old stuff in there: All sorts of old papers, a medal her father got during a war, and the birth certificates of her three children. She didn't have a birth certificate herself---I don't think they had them when she was born, they usually just wrote your name and date in the family Bible. If they found that footlocker with all the papers and pictures, there would be a lot of questions. Maybe it's a bad idea keeping it, but none of us could stand the thought of losing those old momentos.

When I was a child, Grandma was a lot more lucid. She was in the hospital but she had a lot more good days than she does now. Grandma told me stories about how worried she was that Billy Junior would be killed in Germany just like his father had been. Our family has lost quite a few people to war: Great-grandpa died in Germany or France. There was Uncle Mike who died in Vietnam and three of Grandma's uncles died in the Civil War. She told Grandpa Billy that she remembered one of the uncles but it is doubtful seeing as she would have been two when he was killed. Grandma still tells stories about the old days. Her short-term memory is gone but she remembers the house her and Billy Junior's grandfather were living in when William went off to fight the Germans. I know these recollections are true from the stories Billy Junior told me when I was a kid and from the papers in that footlocker. They bought that house for $3000. $3000, for a house! Can't even get a decent car for $3000 these days.

Listen, I know the situation with Grandma is hard for you. I know you don't want to see her, don't even want to talk about her, but she's your Grandma and she loves you. She's your family and how many people have the opportunity to spend time with their great-great-great grandmother? I remember how much you loved US History in school; Grandma could tell you some amazing stories on one of her good days. I remember one she told me about when the US was fighting in Cuba and William tried to run away from home to join the war. He was just a little kid, but he still wanted to fight the Spanish because they had sank some ship---

I don't remember the name of the ship, but it was a big deal back then. Grandma has all sorts of stories like that; firsthand accounts of the Depression and how her first time voting was for Calvin Coolidge because great-great granddad wouldn't let her vote in 1920 right before he died. I'm surprised she never remarried but I guess it was for the best; losing another husband would have been sad for her.

I know this whole situation is weird. Believe me, I have struggled with it myself just like your grandfather and Great Aunt Jill struggled with it...at the end of the day Grandma is family and we have to look after her. I don't know if things will change, she really hasn't aged much since I was a little boy. Chances are she could be your responsibility when I get too old to look after her...

I hope you can do this for me when the time comes, *if* the time comes.

Just think about it, okay? Love, Dad

Eric

Und

Kurdt

Kurt Cobain sees 50

Seattle's second most legendary musician reflects on supper clubs, the short tragic life of Eric Clapton, and the importance of being a father.

Article by Malick Strom for ROLLING STONE on-line

Kurt Cobain sits on a wicker loveseat and sips herbal tea. A frigid breeze rolls in from the Puget Sound and he pulls his cardigan closer.

"I keep having these weird dreams about Eric Clapton," he rasps, reaching for the pack of Winstons on the table next to him. "I'm in this dark museum and there are all these weird paintings and old guitars on display."

He taps out a cigarette, puts it in the center of his mouth, and lights it.

"I'm walking around looking for an exit," he continues, the cigarette bobbing. "But the place is like a maze and I just get more and more lost. I ended up in a corridor that dead ended at this huge picture of Eric Clapton that was lit from below making him look like a god or a demon."

Kurt takes a deep drag and gazes out across the water.

"It's weird: Why the fuck am I dreaming about Eric Clapton?"

Kurt Cobain is not supposed to be smoking; he promised his doctor that he'd stop on his fiftieth birthday but found it even harder than kicking heroin. In the end, he settled for *cutting down*. During the interview Cobain smoked a total of four Winstons. Each time he lit up, the singer would give me a knowing look and rasp, "My cancer is hungry."

I told him that he needed to write a song with that title and Cobain smiled a surprisingly boyish grin.

Kurt doesn't do a lot of interviews. A cynic would say it's because few people care about the former leader of Nirvana anymore. Others would suggest that the singer avoids them. I would propose a third reason: All the rules Cobain's manager lays out in writing that any prospective interviewer has to sign. The biggest one---(it was even in a larger font)---was that I was not allowed to ask any questions about Frances Bean Cobain. Although she is rumored to be well now and leading a good life, it is still a subject her father prefers not to discuss. It is ironic that his daughter's emotional problems caused Kurt Cobain to get past his own issues; that and a potent antidepressant known as Lithia 17. The former tortured lead singer of Nirvana now spends his days in his Japanese inspired home painting or creating eccentric dioramas. Every couple of years he departs for a truncated tour with a band comprised of hired guns.

"Half of them have beards now," Cobain winces. "Two years ago they looked normal, but when we met for rehearsals a couple of weeks ago...beards."

The singer shakes his head, grabs the Winstons, and then sets them down.

"Maybe they moved to Aberdeen," he sighs. "I can't look at them when I'm singing, hippies make me laugh."

I attended one of the dates on his 2015 tour. The band was seated as they played sedate versions of the songs by Cobain's legendary band and from his four solo albums. Some old fans have written him off for the mellow—(some would say *lethargic*)---versions of songs once brimming with pain and anger, some are just glad he got past his angst and self-inflicted torment to see his child grow up. Due to the rules of the contract, I do not share that observation.

Kurt Cobain's dreams about Eric Clapton are not without a degree of eeriness: The legendary guitarist died on Kurt's sixth birthday, February 20, 1973. His death by heroin overdose came as no surprise to anyone who had been watching the guitarist sink deeper into addiction. Clapton's last work, the twisted and searing *Layla and Other Assorted Love Songs*, is seen as a masterwork, one of the best rock albums in the history of the genre.

"Clapton was intense," Cobain says, looking up with a sparkle in his eyes. "People who dismiss Layla and the other songs as mustache cock-rock are idiots. I mean, listen to Bell Bottom Blues; that song is almost *too* real."

He gazes back out at the water and shakes his head.

"I wonder what he'd be like at 50--would he be some sad old man playing lethargic versions of songs that were once totally passionate and intense?"

Cobain taps out another Winston and smiles cryptically.

"Better to die in a blaze of glory, I guess," he says softly.

Kurt takes a sip of tea and watches a gray and white cat prowling the yard for a couple of moments.

"I can totally relate to that album," he continues. "I have had like ten copies of it that I have worn out or lost. That was 1992-1994 for me, maybe beyond that."

The singer takes a long drag and looks over at a plum tree before continuing.

"When Frances started having her problems all my stupid shit just became irrelevant. Even my stomach problem went away because I had to be her dad, you know?"

He looks directly at me and I see why everyone comments about how blue his eyes are. Possibly feeling vulnerable after sharing so much, Cobain looks over at the tree again and then at the Puget Sound in the distance.

"The stronger antidepressants helped, I guess," he continues. "But more so it was someone I love needing me."

He trails off and seems to be watching a ferry crossing the water.

"Crap, that reminds me: I have to go pack and take care of some things before we get on the road tomorrow. More supper clubs," he winces and then shakes his head.

I ask him why he does it if he doesn't enjoy it.

"Ah, I enjoy it once I'm on stage," he grunts. "Sometimes I think about how a Nirvana fan might see it, an old guy playing a young man's songs."

He takes a short drag, the smell of cigarette smoke mixing with the scent of chamomile.

"I'll be doing the new version of You Know You're Right which was originally filled with as much angst as Layla or Bell Bottom Blues..."

He trails off and looks at the cigarette in his hand.

"I don't feel that anymore," Cobain says softly. "I play the songs and I appreciate they're good songs but the emotion that caused their creation is something I can't relate to anymore. That's why we do all these mellow, acoustic versions now; it would just seem false to play them amplified with me screaming over the top. The *why*?"

He shakes his head and snubs his cigarette out. I notice that the bottom of the ashtray has a Guns 'n' Roses logo but someone has changed the "R" into a "P."

"Well, there are still lawsuits, pending, you know?" Kurt says. "Some of the stuff that Frances has done, some stuff having to do with Courtney."

He looks over at the gray and white cat.

"I've got to get ready now," Cobain says this so softly it's like he's talking to himself or a ghost. "Time for me to get my velvet jacket and cummerbund out of the closet---have you seen my truss? That, of course, will be track three on the next album: Have You Seen My Truss? The cover will have me seated at a low table with a big grin on my face as I look down at an overflowing fondue pot. It'll be a concept album about cheese, very hot cheese."

Kurt Cobain rises slowly and makes his way back into the house, I do not follow him in.

In Seattle I got lost and found it impossible to use the GPS in my rental while driving. I parked and looked for someplace to get directions. Passing an alley, I saw a young woman spray-painting something on a brick wall. She either did not sense my presence or didn't care. When she was done the artist dramatically tossed the aerosol can aside and stood back to admire her handiwork: *Clapton is God.*

"Big Clapton fan?" I asked.

She jumped at the sound of my voice.

"Yeah. I wished I could have done this four days ago on the anniversary, but I had the flu."

The anniversary---the day the guitarist was found dead next to a garden bench.

"Your parents were probably in grammar school when he died," I suggested.

The painter was thin and had her long, blonde hair parted in the center. She licked a finger and smoothed one of the letters before answering.

"They don't even know about him," the girl frowned. "I had an uncle who turned me onto Clapton. It's what I listen to when I feel like shit."

I tell her about my job and that I had just spent a couple of hours with Kurt Cobain.

"What a sell out," she said, rolling her eyes. "Talk about someone who should have died young. Did you see that unplugged concert he did on MTV3 last year? Serve the Servants used to be this incredible, angry song but there he was crooning it like Tony Bennett and limply strumming an acoustic guitar. He had a bassoon player with him, a fucking bassoon player on Scentless Apprentice! It was sick, there was all this passion in the stuff he was doing twenty-five years ago but it's totally gone now."

That night I had a dream that I was walking into Kurt Cobain's garden for another interview but it was Eric Clapton sitting on the loveseat, an Eric Clapton that had lived to see 50. We chatted a bit about records he would never make and achievements that would never be his. I awoke feeling empty and depressed. In his twenties, Eric Clapton was suffering through two unrequited love affairs: One for his best friend's wife and the other for heroin. He made a beautiful, tormented album under an assumed name and then decided it'd be a good idea to wash down some dangerously pure heroin with whisky. The end result has been the source of discussion and debate the past forty-four years. I think of Kurt's dream, of a small somewhat faded man looking up at the larger than life portrait of one of his dead heroes---

I think of that scene and feel sorry for both of them.

umschlungen umschlungen umschlungen umschlungen umschlungen umschlungen
umschlungen umschlungen umschlungen umschlungen umschlungen umschlungen
umschlungen umschlungen umschlungen umschlungen umschlungen umschlungen
umschlungen umschlungen umschlungen umschlungen umschlungen umschlungen
umschlungen umschlungen umschlungen umschlungen umschlungen umschlungen
umschlungen umschlungen umschlungen umschlungen umschlungen umschlungen
umschlungen umschlungen umschlungen umschlungen umschlungen umschlungen
umschlungen umschlungen umschlungen umschlungen umschlungen umschlungen
umschlungen umschlungen umschlungen umschlungen umschlungen umschlungen

thick

I sat in her bed unsure what to do; she had clearly not gotten off and everything I tried seemed to have an effect. Elaine was frustrated and it made me frustrated.

"What do you need?" I asked.

She looked over at me. I saw the frustration I had been picking up on but I also saw other emotions: Embarrassment. Hurt. Guilt.

Her vagina had felt *loose*, that's as best as I can explain it; maybe she was used to really endowed men, maybe that was the only way she could get off; I have never had any complaints but I know I am just average in that regard.

Elaine lay back and seemed to be studying the pebbled surface of the ceiling. Her hands made fists and squeezed the top of the sheet. The silence was a weight and I wanted it off.

"Look...if you're into really big guys I get it..."

"It's not that," she said sharply.

Clearly she was sensitive about whatever was going on with her. I went from confused to awkward and then resentful; I had offered to go down on her, had wanted to, but she had grabbed at my head.

"Don't, okay?" She said to the ceiling.

"Okay..."

"I'm okay," she smiled. "You don't..."

The smile had left Elaine's face.

"I'm just not into it...."

"No need to explain—"

"I don't know, it weirds me out, like you could start chewing on me, keep going until you get to my guts...I know how crazy that must sound."

"No, no, I get it," It sounded fucking nuts.

Ten minutes later we were sitting in her bed surrounded by a silence that was anything but comfortable. It seemed a good idea to leave; if she wanted to talk Elaine would have however long it took me to put on my clothes. I started to get out of bed, she grabbed my arm.

"Please stay, I really don't want you to go..."

"Okay—"

"At least I didn't piss the bed this time," she said quietly.

What could I say to that? I got back under the blankets with her, Elaine took my hand.

"This always happens," she said. "Lots of times I will pee in the bed."

"Lots of people are incontinent, I get it—"

"No, you don't," she squeezed my hand. "I told you that I was married before, right?"

"Yeah, I remember you mentioning it."

Elaine closed her eyes, her face was troubled; had her husband abused her? God, what if he did something horrible like made her have sex with a donkey?

"Joe had lost an arm when he was a kid," she said. "He had a dirt bike and was racing it. He wiped out and damaged his arm so much they had to amputate it. By that time I met him, he had worn a prosthetic for fifteen years, you wouldn't even know it watching him."

She rolled on her side to look at me so I rolled onto my left side to meet her gaze. Her eyes were bright green, lovely eyes. Her skin was perfect, as well. I had been secretly crushing on her for sometime and had been surprised when she had leaned over to kiss me that afternoon.

"Joe and I started dating," she continued. "We became serious pretty fast. He had gotten blood poisoning after his accident, nearly died; he explained to me that he didn't waste time, didn't fuck around, because he understood how close death really was....to all of us."

"Makes sense after a situation like that."

I saw the shape of her breasts though the sheet and wanted to touch one. I reached under the covers to caress her right breast, toy with her nipple using my right index finger. Elaine laughed a little, smiled, bit her lip, and then grabbed my right hand to hold it; playtime was over.

"Joe had always wanted to do something," she continued, massaging the fingers of my right hand with her left one. "Oh, he looked so nervous when he asked...he was scared because no other girl had agreed to what he wanted. In fact, those relationships ended the day he asked. I told Joe I would try. I mean, I didn't see how what he wanted was possible, but I really loved him and could see that it meant a lot to him."

She rolled over to grab the glass of water off her nightstand. Elaine took a drink and handed the glass to me. I drank. She had stopped talking, looked nervous, probably about the rest of her story and how I would react to it.

"Joe had always wanted to make love to a girl..."

Elaine stopped, I could tell she was determined and screwing up her courage.

"He wanted to do it with his stump."

I managed to keep a straight face. Thinking of my own arm, it sounded...difficult. Of course, women give birth to babies—a baby is bigger than a stump, right?

"This must sound really freaky..."

"No, no, I've heard much stranger," it sounded pretty freaky.

"We lubed up his stump, and Joe was very gentle, but it was too thick at first, it was too much...it really hurt."

"How did the stump feel?"

Elaine looked at me as if my question was strange but after a couple of seconds her expression became thoughtful.

"The end felt like bread dough."

"Oh," I imagined the Pillsbury Doughboy trying to fuck her with a white stump and struggled to keep a straight face.

"I could see how disappointed he was that first time, so we kept trying. Eventually I could take it and he fucked with me with his stump until I came."

"What about him?"

"He was so excited he jerked off with his intact arm in a couple of seconds."

I nodded as if someone was telling me a story about learning how to use a complicated stereo system or how to manage a sailboat.

"So...what happened to you two? It sounds like you loved him."

Misery clouded Elaine's face, she hiccuped and tears rolled out of her eyes. I took both her hands in mine.

"He wasn't true to me," Elaine said eventually. "He had another girl he was fucking—"

"With his stump?"

Elaine nodded vigorously but didn't cry anymore.

"I'm telling you this because I really like you, Ike, and I want you to understand, you know?"

She rolled over to face me again. Using my thumb, I wiped her tears away and she smiled at that. I was mad at Joe; Elaine was such a lovely person, she had endured a lot to make him happy and in the end he had cheated on her.

"I want to work on this with you," I said. "They have really big dildos out there, I'm sure we could find one large enough to get you off."

She tucked her chin in to stop meeting my eyes.

"I have one I'm just..."

Elaine laughed a little, pulled her hands free and covered her face with them.

"I'm kinda embarrassed by Billy Dee—"

"Billy Dee?"

"That's what I call it."

I made the connection that Billy Dee was a dildo.

"I want to meet Billy Dee," I said, pulling her hands away and looking in her eyes.

Elaine looked at me intently, probably trying to read if I was making fun or not. When she saw I wasn't, she smiled happily, and leaned over to get something from underneath the bed. As she did, I stuck my index finger in the very top of her ass crack after wetting it. Elaine cried out in surprise and then started laughing.

"Stop that! I almost fell off the bed!"

She rolled back up with the largest dildo I had ever seen. It wasn't black, it was blue and the manufacturer hadn't tried to give it details of a normal penis; it was just an enormous blue dildo.

"Ike, meet Billy Dee."

"Nice to meet you, Billy Dee," I said, shaking the tip.

That busted Elaine up, she rolled over to get a bottle of lube from her nightstand. She started rubbing the lube onto Billy Dee and smiled at me.

"This could be the beginning of a beautiful friendship," she said.

R Kelly

(& The Winchester Closet of Mystery)

This story began one week ago…

Booting up the news after I started my coffee, I read that R. Kelly had died in his sleep at the age of 92; he had passed on before I could finish my interviews with him for a long piece. I sent a message to my editor advising him of a possible alteration to our plans and then drank my coffee.

With Kelly's death it would have been logical to assume that there will never be a 1,234th episode of the *In the Closet* series, that after 55 years the on-going story had ended with Kelly's last breath. The singer had never shared his reasons for carrying on the series so long; I asked about them near the end of the first interview and a few times during the second but he was evasive: He feigned weariness or senility, one time he soiled his pants to distract me. During our last meeting I thought he was asleep and gently grabbed his arm. An ebony claw, much more powerful than I would have suspected, grabbed my own arm and his eyes became alert, probing---

And fearful. His expression changed from terror to cunning and the singer smiled a little, it wasn't a nice smile, it was a feral smile.

"It will get you now," he said.

Unnerved, I asked for clarification.

"They've seen you talkin' to me," he nodded, his eyes cold but gleeful. "It will get you, now, *yes it will.*"

Those were the last words R. Kelly said to me.

I need help. R. Kelly didn't take care of me. I thought he was my man, you know? I thought we were bros even though I was his valet but he didn't do shit for me. That's cold man. I can help with your interview if you can help me out a bit: I'm old, man, I need some help.

--message from Tyrell "Flipper" Percy

Flipper had been R. Kelly's valet the last thirty-four years of the singer's life. He had succeeded his father Jimmy "Flip" Percy who had been R. Kelly's first personal assistant. Flipper met me at a YepperDeppers near the cheap hotel he had a room in. The valet had moved there after being evicted from R. Kelly's mansion the same day his boss perished. I found the former assistant to be a small, threadbare man with a weary ring of gray hair and matching beard. He would be best described as an equal mixture of sighs and resentment.

"It was *cold*, man," he said to me plaintively. "I treated R good, ya know what I'm saying? I took *care* of him...I was loyal, man, and he kicked me to the curb like a ten-dollar bitch, man...it was *cold*."

I agreed to help him and transferred a couple hundred to his account as we sipped our coffee. He poured an obscene amount of creamer and sugar in his.

"Need the calories, man," he muttered. "R didn't leave me shit."

I sipped my own coffee, not meeting his stare, trying to not to fuel his bitterness.

"You said in your message you had some big news for me," I probed.

Flipper's eyes widened a little. He glanced around the restaurant warily before leaning towards me across the table; apparently, in his state of poverty the old man had been unable to buy soap.

"This is dangerous for me," The assistant whispered. "A lot of people...there's lots of weird people out there, you know? *In the Closet* has become very important to them, folks in cults and shit like that."

He read something in my eyes and the fear on his face was replaced by resentment.

"Don't worry, I ain't wantin' no more money after this. I don't give a shit if they kill me, to be honest; ain't got much of a life since R left me in the lurch."

He took another sip of his coffee and looked sad.

"That was *cold*, man," Flipper continued. "I was helping R work on the last couple hundred chapters and he just kicked me to the curb."

The older man shook some of his bitterness off and focused on me.

"I was 13 when the story started. My dad was R's closest employee and I hung out with him from time to time when I wasn't living with my moms. Pop didn't tell me much about the series until right before he died when I was like 35 or 30 or somethin' like that---"

"34," I corrected him gently.

"Heh heh, you smart with the math, man. Stick to the math; the math will make you rich, make you your own man so no one can do nothin' cold to you."

"Your father told you the story before he died?" I said, attempting to get him back on track.

"Yeah, my poppa died young. He was only in his fifties. Smoked three packs a day. R took care of my pops and took me on as a valet when poppa got too sick to look after RK. I was visiting pops in the hospital when R stopped by. It was that day they told me about what led to *In the Closet* becoming such a long ass story."

Flipper stopped abruptly when the waitress came by to refill our cups. Once again, he dumped a mountain of sugar and creamer into his coffee; enough that I was surprised the cup didn't overflow. The assistant watched the waitress go and didn't continue until he was sure she was out of earshot.

"A couple of years before they started shooting the story," Flipper continued. "R was in all sorts of trouble because he made a film of him and some under-aged girl. R spent months praying and asking the Lord how he could repent, but he didn't get no signs. A few more months passed and he started work on *In the Closet*, cutting some rough demos at home. It was no big deal at first, just something RK was fucking around with. Desperate to figure out a way to get out from under his troubles, R went to a spiritualist who saw that my man was working on a story, saw that shit in the cards or something, and told RK that the day he stopped working on the story, he would die and would be sent someplace to answer for his sins. This freaked R out and he became obsessed with *In the Closet*—he stopped working on other music projects, everything became focused on *In the Closet*. At first, it was just this six part soap opera, but then it went on: 12 chapters. 22 chapters. 50 chapters. 250 chapters. Up until ten years ago or so, R was working on the story seven days a week, nearly every day of the year, either sketching out storyboards or shooting the chapters or...*anything*. Even if he wrote a single line of dialogue in a day, he felt he was working and his life would be spared and it was, up to three days ago."

Flipper heard a noise outside: He jerked in the booth as his eyes popped wide open; a few moments later I smelled the pungent odor of urine.

"Damn; They have to be close," he said, his voice like a stretched band. "They think I know, They think because R and I are close, *were* close---shit, no we weren't close; him kicking me out like that. How could I think we were close after shit like that, man?"

"Maybe he told his lawyer to evict you immediately to make you look unimportant," I suggested. "Maybe R. Kelly was trying to save you."

Flipper looked over at me with an uncomfortable degree of sadness; I was certain he was about to cry.

"Damn, maybe that's true. Maybe I'm being harsh on R for no reason."

He looked thoughtful, ground some tears in his right eye with a fist, and then shook his head ruefully

"It don't matter," he smiled bitterly. "None of this will fool Them."

"Them?"

"Them, the weirdos," Flipper said impatiently. "The people who have been obsessed with *In the Closet* pretty much since it came out. They will come after me because They think I know the secrets like how *In the Closet* was supposed to end."

"How *was* it supposed to end?"

"I don't fucking know, man!" Flipper shouted.

Realizing he had drawn attention to himself, the former assistant shrank down in the booth, eyes wide and frightened until he determined no one had looked over.

"There is no ending, man," he continued quietly, shaking his head. "R was scared to even consider an ending because it would mean the end of his life."

Flipper took a sip of his coffee and glanced around the diner as I probed him further.

"Even in his last days when he was in a wheelchair and his heart condition was getting progressively worse he was still working?" I asked. "He seemed sick when I met him in person and sounded terrible over the phone when I tried to make another interview appointment."

"Even then," Flipper nodded solemnly. "He couldn't face death because he feared punishment for what he had done. R always felt the Lord never spoke to him anymore because the Lord couldn't forgive his sins so he never planned an ending, he never planned a resolution. I mean, we had 1234 through 1237 sketched out and he was mumbling a bit about 1238 and 1239, but it was just supposed to go on, man; just go on and on and on."

"Can't you tell the people following you, that?"

There was another strange noise in the parking lot. Flipper looked terrified and climbed out of the booth. As I had suspected, the front of his cheap slacks were darkened by urine at the crotch and spreading down the right leg.

"They won't believe me, man," he stammered. "They think I know the secret, that RK told me the ending and They won't rest until they try to pry out of me---They'll probably go all *Marathon Man* on my ass or some shit like that."

He bent down to grab his coffee cup; Flipper's hands were so shaky he nearly dropped it. The old man took a sip and set it down with a clatter.

"I'm a dead man," he said to me quietly. "In a way, it's a fuckin' relief..."

Flipper looked down at me, saw something, and smiled with a cunning I would not have imagined possible on his befuddled face; it reminded me of the expression on R. Kelly's face during our last interview.

"Maybe you're the ticket to my freedom, man," Flipper nodded. And he was gone before elaborating; a man with a fear of an ending but not the ending everyone sought and would be forced to keep seeking.

But the story wasn't over.

There was one thing that Flipper had chosen not to tell me, not directly, at least:

Maybe you're the ticket to my freedom, man.

It took me a few hours to figure out what he had meant: Maybe the people watching him would think he had passed the secrets onto *me*.

I laughed at myself the first time I considered that…it isn't quite as funny now: People across streets and on the other end of trains seem to be looking at me. When I notice Them, They pointedly look away. Things in my apartment have gone missing, other things have been moved around.

Understanding there was no other choice, I left this status on my MEMEME profile:

Tomorrow, the Story continues.

Hopefully it will buy me some time, buy me some peace.

In the meantime, I have a story to work on.

das haben sie nicht kommen sehen das haben sie nicht kommen sehen

das haben sie nicht kommen sehen

das haben sie nicht kommen sehen

das haben sie nicht kommen sehen

das haben sie nicht kommen sehen

das haben sie nicht kommen sehen

Clause 134C

das haben sie nicht kommen sehen

das haben sie nicht kommen sehen

das haben sie nicht kommen sehen

das haben sie nicht kommen sehen

das haben sie nicht kommen sehen

das haben sie nicht kommen sehen

1

"They gave me a bird once; a beautiful, green bird."

Mick's voice was soft as he looked out the window. He was talking, that was a good thing, but he looked sad which was not good. There was a meet and greet in an hour; he needed to look like a rock star and not some sad old man talking about some fucking bird.

"What kind of bird was it?" Hati, his minder asked,"A parrot?"

Mick smiled a little and turned away from the window but did not look at Hati.

"It wasn't a parrot. To be honest, I have no idea what sort of bird it was but it was beautiful."

The Dresser had no idea what to do or say so he just stood there, waiting for whatever was on Mick's mind to run its course.

Sometimes he hated his job. The pay was good and there were side benefits but there was pressure, a lot of pressure. If you screwed up in a noodle shop, you'd get yelled at. If you screwed up as Mick's Dresser...well, who knew what Turner would do to you.

"That green bird used to hop around its cage and fly from perch to perch," Mick continued. "After a few years, it stopped hopping around and stuck to one branch---you could tell it wasn't moving because its shit was in one place. One morning, I found it lying dead in its cage on top of that pile of shit....that beautiful, green bird."

What was the right face after such a story? Sad? Amused? Hati had no idea, no fucking idea whatsoever. Now there were fifty-six minutes until the meet and greet and Mick needed to be made up and dressed. By that point, they should have had his hair touched up, not be chatting about some stupid bird. What could you do? Mick was the Star.

All I did was wish him a happy birthday. If I had known it would lead to this, the sad face and all the talk about some fucking dead bird, I would have kept my mouth shut.

Hati looked uncomfortable to Mick; he appeared awkward and angry---just another stupid, impatient young man. It wasn't his fault, he had no idea what was really going on, but he was still part of it; he worked for the people who had made Mick a prisoner. The Star could tell when people were sincere and when people were just kissing his ass; he had experienced a lot of the latter and not enough of the former in his life---too many years and too much bullshit. Hati didn't care if he had a happy birthday, he just wanted Mick to make his job easier. He appeased the star and complimented him in exchange for cooperation.

Fuck him.

"I've been told that this is the best penthouse in the city, 143rd floor and all---what do you think, Hati?"

"It's a great place, incredible view."

Mick walked back to the window and tapped on the thick glass. It was unbreakable, one of the precautions.

"Did they tell you what happened to your predecessor?" He asked.

Hati struggled to hide his impatience.

"Predecessor?"

"The person who did your job before you did it," Mick explained.

"No. I do not know what happened."

Hati may not have known the details but the Minder knew it was bad; Mick could tell by the nervousness in Hati's eyes.

"He served me some food that had peppers in it, spicy ones, could have been Ghost Peppers or Habaneros, I have no idea. My stomach can't handle that sort of thing anymore and I had to go to the hospital. I was down for two weeks, missed a performance...Turner wasn't happy."

"I imagine not."

Hati no longer sounded nervous, he sounded as if every muscle in his body was pulled taut and he was about to vomit. Mick couldn't look at him, knew he would start giggling if he did.

"Turner took him up on the roof for a chat," the star continued. "One moment the three of us were in this living room having a conversation, and then Turner said 'Excuse me, Mick, I need to speak with Lon for a moment.' A couple of minutes later, I see Lon flying by the window."

"Falling?" Hati could barely get the word out. He looked like he was about to shit his pants. No, his arsehole was probably so puckered, such a thing was probably impossible.

"Um hmm," The singer looked away so his smile wasn't visible. "You know, I wonder what happens when you hit the pavement from such a height: Would it leave a crater in the cement or would you just splatter?"

"I don't know."

Mick turned to his minder. with a sly smile.

"Well, hopefully you won't find out."

Forty minutes later, Mick was sitting in his dressing room alone. He had been an asshole to Hati but Hati should have known better than to remind him it was July 26th. Thinking about his birthday made him think about how old he was and thinking about how old he was reminded him of *everything*. Turner had brought the bird to the penthouse shortly after Mick had been moved in. The bird was smart and hated its cage, always crashing into the bars or pecking at them. When it first saw Mick in the morning it would start shrieking, probably to be let out or maybe just to let Mick know how pissed off it was.

Yeah, you and I both, bird.

A tap on the door---*ten minutes.*

Mick rolled his eyes and opened his laptop to brush up on his past.

Thank God for Wikipedia.

They always asked random, obscure questions---how was he supposed to remember that shit? Who gave a fuck who was the second engineer on *Goats Head Soup*? What was the inspiration for "Happy?"

I didn't even sing on that tune; I don't know, Keith was probably happy or something, no fucking clue.

Keith. Lucky bastard.

Well, lucky for him, not so lucky for his family and friends.

Keith was the reason Mick was not allowed to have knives in the apartment.

"Fuckers didn't see that coming, did they?" Mick smiled at his Wikipedia page.

If Lon was tossed off a roof for making Mick sick, who knew what happened to Keith's Dresser. The singer knew what fate a few of Keith's relatives met, Turner had sent him pictures; they were ugly, full of pain and death.

The smile left Mick's face and he closed the laptop.

Another tap on the door---*five minutes.*

You're supposed to be on top of this shit, how did you miss this, Mick?

Keith years earlier, angry, pacing and knocking things off the table—he tried to throw a chair but the effort winded him.

Clause 134C---how did you and the lawyers miss that? How is it even fucking legal?

It was. As absurd as it seemed, Clause 134C was perfectly legal. Turner had explained the specifics and Mick was savvy enough to understand them...

But not savvy enough to pick up on that when going over the contract. It had been a bad time in his life and he had been distracted: L'Wren had died a few days earlier. He had assumed it was just a normal contract, he had assumed that everyone knew not to try and slip any shit past him---

And this is where assuming got me, got all of us and our families.

The day of Keith's tantrum was very clear in his memory. They were still free back then. A meeting had been called by their management company. Someone named Turner had taken over their affairs and wanted to meet with them in New York. Keith wasn't doing so good by that point, barely walking even with the use of a cane. What could you expect from a 90 year old man? Even Ronnie had lost some of his energy---some.

"What's this about, Mick?" Ronnie had asked.

They were always expecting him to know. Sometimes he enjoyed being the one who held the information, sometimes it was exhausting. At that moment, it was exhausting and he felt all 91 years he had lived.

"No idea. I am assuming they are going to go over our numbers for the year or something."

"But it's only October, a bit early isn't it?" Ronnie with that annoying half-witted stare of his.

"Like I said, I have no idea."

The conference room door opened and a man walked in. He was white and somewhere in his thirties wearing an expensive looking suit and smile like a used car salesman and---

Some odd energy, something unusual and probably dangerous, almost like a wild animal; I remember picking it up in those first moments.

A more urgent tap on the door---*one minute.*

There was no more time for going over things that troubled him, it was showtime.

2

Mick Jagger thought he knew about money. He believed that he had seen all you could do if you had a vast amount of resources: Hundreds of millions of American dollars. The reverence of millions of rock and rock fans including the leaders of nations. In his mind, he perceived that he had reached the limits of the power a private citizen could hold---

He had been wrong and, in the end, had been embarrassed by his arrogance and naivety.

"You okay, Mick?"

Words bringing him into the present; concerned tone of voice and matching face. The man he was talking to was the CEO of one of the bigger banks---was it Chase? Wells Fargo? Mick couldn't remember.

"Yeah, yeah, sorry--what was your question?"

And they went on chatting as if the situation were perfectly normal. This guy wanted to know about Jerry Hall, probably was curious what it had been like to fuck her but was too timid to ask. Most questions were not off limits, it was part of the package people like the CEO bought into. The only rule was that all inquiries could not relate to the past eighteen years.

"No offense," the CEO continued. "But Charlie was always my favorite Stone. There was something quirky about him, you know?"

Quirky? What the fuck do you know about quirky? You have to be one of the four most dull people in the world.

"Ah, yes, good old Charlie," Mick forced a smile.

"I remember when he died, I was in college..."

Something on Mick's face made the CEO stop, look worried.

"Is that one of the things I can't ask about?" The CEO asked.

"No, no...it's fine. Yes, Charlie was a lovely man, no doubt."

I saw you at the last performance. How can you talk about Charlie being dead when you saw him on stage a week ago?

He wanted to ask that but such questions were not allowed; Turner would not tolerate anyone fucking with The Illusion.

Speak of the devil...possibly.

Turner had appeared out of nowhere, smiling and touching the CEO on the shoulder.

"I apologize Bob but Mick is getting a bit tired and needs to rest."

The CEO looked from Turner to Mick as if he understood---of course he *didn't*, that would have been impossible. Mick got up and walked with Turner to the elevator, his personal elevator.

"What's up with you today, Mick?"

"Nothing, just a bunch of dull questions answered with aplomb and charm."

"Hati told me you were moping and talking about some bird."

"What do you expect? He wished me a happy birthday. You know I don't like to be reminded of that."

"I'll have a chat with him."

Mick thought about Lon falling past his window, his Dresser had been smiling.

"Well, please don't be too hard on him, I'm sure he meant nothing of it."

Fuck you, you bastards.

Keith. It was horrible to think of him doing that to himself but he was free, wasn't he? Keith had been angry since their first meeting with Turner, the one where he had attempted to throw a tantrum. When their new manager had walked in the guitarist had picked on whatever ominous energy Turner was giving off; he and Mick had instinctively moved closer to one another.

"Great to meet the three of you finally," Turner had said with a smile that could have been mistaken for warm, modest. "Not to sound unprofessional, but I'm a huge fan. I think my favorite album is *Some Girls*, love that one."

"Lovely of you to say." Mick, all charm including an ingratiating smile.

"So...what's this meeting about, then?" Ronnie, looking bewildered and shifting a glass of water from one hand to the other.

"Well, I wanted to feel you guys out about the next tour—" Turner started.

That was as far as he got. Any fear Keith had felt vanished and he got in Turner's face.

"What the fuck are you talking about? Charlie's dead, this isn't fucking 1978, man!"

"I didn't mean to offend you, Keith." Turner's smile became tighter---

Something in his eyes made the guitarist step back, look almost contrite. Mick couldn't see Turner's eyes, but he felt *something*, something *bad*.

"Look, man..." Keith rasped softly. "I get you're a fan, but it isn't the Stones without Charlie. Mick and I have been saying that forever, man. No offense to Ronnie, but it was always the three of us."

Turner just looked at him for a few moments and then began talking. That was when the world ended.

3

Alone in the lift back to the penthouse, Mick thought about the green bird and how it would shriek and peck at the bars of its cage. He would walk over and their eyes would meet.

Yeah, I know I know, but since we're both stuck here would you mind bringing the noise down a bit?

The bird would eventually calm down. It had already accepted its fate, it just seemed to need to remind Mick that it was still upset. When he looked into its eyes he would open himself, Mick could be more open with that bird than he had been with other people. Part was an attempt to let the bird know he got what it was feeling to calm it, part of it was his own need for closeness.

"Quite stupid, of course. It was just a fucking bird." Softly, to himself, in the elevator.

A year after their first meeting with Turner, he and Keith were on a jet flying east. All they knew was that they were headed to one of the biggest cities in Asia...and that the Rolling Stones would be expected to perform. Keith had protested loudly and Mick with a civil firmness, but then the pictures came: One of Keith's personal assistants, hacked up with a machete. An old friend of Mick's shot in the abdomen and bleeding out. A bass playing buddy of

Ronnie's, hung from a tree. All of them had talked to their attorneys and personal managers and everyone they consulting with told them the same thing:

I have no idea how this is legal, but Clause 134C is perfectly legal...and binding.

Mick and Keith had no idea how the management company intended to pursue its legal right, the two of them talked about that in Mick's apartment with the incredible view.

"How do they expect this to work, man?" Keith, drinking from a tall glass of vodka and orange. "I mean, my hands are fucked, I can't really play—will they just have me miming with some hired gun in the wings playing my parts?"

"I don't know," Mick said thoughtfully. "I mean, if they want the Rolling Stones to play then why have they told the world that I'm dead?"

It had been a shock a few weeks earlier when he brought up CNN and saw the headline "Mick Jagger dead at 92."

"Why did they have you die first?" Keith shook his head, lit a cigarette.

"It's all a joke," Mick explained. "They always said you'd outlive us all. Looks like you did."

They both thought of Ronnie and the moment became solemn. Ronnie had been the first one to undergo the Treatments and something had gone wrong, catastrophically wrong. Whatever damage had been done was irreparable, or so Turner had told them.

A few days after that conversation Keith had gotten the first Treatment. He went in weak with his hands too arthritic for him to play guitar. Mick didn't see him for three weeks. He himself had undergone plastic surgery to get his face back to how it looked in his sixties. After twenty-two days, Keith had been brought round to the penthouse.

"Can your guy get me a vodka and orange?" He asked.

"I imagine, they can get you anything you want," Mick replied. "Think of the most unusual thing and they will find it for you. It's quite impressive, really."

"Can they get us the fuck out of here?" The guitarist snarled.

Lon had gone to the kitchen and made Keith's drink. It was perfect down to the brand of vodka and the amount of pulp in the orange juice. Keith took the glass and looked at his hand with awe.

"My hands are like new. They hurt like a bastard for a week but now...I was actually playing a week after I got out, man. It's crazy after all these years of arthritis."

"Yeah, they do amazing things. Have they sent you a schedule?"

"Maybe," Keith grunted. "I don't know."

"We're playing in a week, some sort of theatre gig."

"Us? You and I or us and a band?"

"The Rolling Stones."

Keith had shaken his head and walked over to where the green bird was hopping around in its cage.

"We know what will happen if we say *no*," he said softly, studying the bird. "Clearly, we have to go along with this, but what are we going along with, you know? I mean, Ronnie and Charlie are dead---"

"They'll probably have some pros out there with us. Most people thought of the Stones as you and I, anyway."

My assumptions were perfectly logical. Charlie was dead, Ronnie was dead, and yet we were scheduled to play as the Rolling Stones. I imagined we were going to be trotted out like one of those old R&B acts where only one original member is still in the band. It was the only thing that made sense, not that any of this has ever made any sense.

Back in the present, Mick went and sat at the piano. He wrote songs from time to time, had even recorded a few, not that anyone would ever hear them. Mick Jagger was dead, after all, and the people downstairs only wanted to hear the hits: Brown Sugar. Miss You. Satisfaction, Sympathy for the Devil...it felt weird playing that last one when Turner was around, but what could you do? It was on The List: Sympathy. Jumping Jack Flash. Start Me Up. Nothing after the late 80s. Rain Fall Down had gotten on The List once, but that had been an anomaly. The singer's hands started playing the basic melody from Miss You. His eyes were closed, he was only looking at the past, sitting in the dressing room downstairs with Keith years earlier.

"This whole situation has got me thinking about William Penn." Keith had said, hands moving over his guitar.

"Never heard of him," Mick replied dismissively.

"He was some cat back in the USA a long time ago. When he died they stuffed him and put him in a case."

Mick thought of Ronnie and Charlie and winced; it was the last thing he wanted to hear but Keith was his only friend there--- *Maybe this is Hell. Maybe the two of us are really dead and have forgotten that we died...*

Thinking like that was bad. It could throw you off during the performance which would upset Turner which would lead to more photographs: A cousin with a finger lopped off. An old acquaintance attacked with an iron, hot metal meeting skin.

"How the fuck did this happen, Mick? I mean, we have, *had*, the best lawyers in the world, man..."

Keith trailed off, walking over to a counter to grab his cigarettes.

"Fuck if I know." Mick, staring at the door and sighing.

Back in the present, Mick stopped playing and opened his eyes. *How the fuck did this happen, Mick? I mean, we have the best lawyers in the world, man.*

Whether or not it made sense it had happened and no one could protect them. The realization of their lack of control of their destiny was bad, what happened when they started performing was even worse. Mick walked to the fridge and got a smoothie. Why did he bother eating healthy? He could eat crap and they could negate the effects. He could gorge himself on fatty food and they'd simply put him on a more rigorous exercise regimen or schedule him for liposuction.

I could scar my face, if I had anything to scar it with, and they'd fix that, too.

He was pacing again. Maybe he could talk Turner into another couple of weeks somewhere in the tropics, somewhere with white sand. Be away from the city and all the lights and noise. Of course there would be bodyguards everywhere---even ones below the surface of the sea---but it'd be good to be a beach again or anyplace other than the city and the penthouse.

A little after nine, there was a message from Turner. Mick got nervous every time one came in; the possibility of more pictures. There were photos in the message, but they were benign: The Edith Grove replica was finished. The singer clicked through the photographs and marvelled at the accuracy right down what looked like spit on the walls and filthy dishes in the sink.

"What a shithole," he smiled despite himself.

We're excited about this exhibit, the message that accompanied the photos read. *We are even piping in how we imagine the place smelled, farts and dirty socks and rotten food.*

Mick looked over the pictures again. How had they gotten it so exact? There were loads of stories out there about Edith Grove, but details were always left out or forgotten or both; things that only one living person knew. The more he thought about it, the more unsettling the pictures became.

What if that's because these pictures are some sort of window to 1962 or whenever it was? What if Keith, Brian, and I are just out scrounging for change for the fucking heater or something?

Unnerved, Mick closed the email and got up from his desk. He was pretty sure that he hadn't died, but it wasn't a hundred percent certainty.

You'd have to remember something as big as dying, right?

"Stop it, just stop it."

He wouldn't allow himself to think about that sort of thing. That sort of thinking could drive you mad.

4

Four weeks after arriving in a large city they didn't know the name of, Mick and Keith played their first concert. Mick was brought down from his penthouse to a theatre located on the bottom levels of the same building. He had no idea where Keith lived---the topic had never come up between the two of them---but the singer assumed it was the same building. Keith was already in the dressing room, absentmindedly riffing on Micawber or a Telecaster that looked exactly like Micawber....

It was hard to tell what was real and what was a replica.

After a nod to his bandmate, Mick went into the next room to do his vocal warm-ups. He had no idea why he was bothering; they were there against their will, prisoners, why even bother to put on a decent show? It wasn't just the fear of more pictures, it was something else. His thoughts had been interrupted by the sound of a bass guitar being tested and then a clavinet.

"They're playing Heartbreaker." Keith nodded.

"Or trying to." Mick, smirking.

They looked at each other: Enemies, friends, brothers, the *other half*.

"Remember when we were putting together *A Bigger Bang* and it was just the two of us?" Mick mused.

Keith looked disgusted, shook his head.

"This is not the same; Charlie was just sick, we were just biding time until he came back. Out there, it's just going to be a bunch of strangers, not the fucking same at all."

"I didn't suggest it was the same," Mick replied. "I was just thinking about that album."

And what if Charlie is out there, waiting for us? Charlie and Ronnie and Bill and Brian and Stu.

It was a terrifying thought and Mick struggled to will it away.

"This is going to be a charade, man." Keith, looking angry as he played a slow blues run. "It's going to fuck the whole Rolling Stones thing up---what if they release a video or recording of it? Us fucking playing without Charlie or Ronnie and calling ourselves the Stones?"

"I don't think they'll do that."

"Yeah, well you missed that fucking clause, too."

Ten minutes later they were walking down a short hallway to the stage. The backing musicians---a keyboardist, two female singers, and a bass player---were back by the curtain. On the main stage...

"Fuck me." Keith, stopping in his tracks and unable to go any further.

Ronnie and Charlie were waiting for them...or two objects that looked like Ronnie and Charlie.

"Interesting." Mick, also stopped on the edge of the stage, not wanting to get any closer.

Both of their bandmates were wearing sunglasses and Mick had the feeling it was because they didn't have eyes.

So...what are they? Robots? Their skin stretched over robots? Them reanimated?

Turner had appeared beside them.

"You guys excited? First show in a long time, right."

"Uh, I can't do this." Mick, fixated on the accuracy of Charlie's hair down to the bald spot.

"Yeah...no." Keith, swaying a bit in place.

Turner just smiled at them.

"Come on, guys, this is a big night: *The Stones*!"

"This isn't the Stones," Keith said evenly. "I have no fucking idea what this is, but this isn't the Stones. It's us and robots that look like the Stones."

"Robots is not entirely accurate---"

"I don't fucking care," Keith snarled.

The smile left Turner's face.

"Look, I don't want to be the bad guy, that's why we've left your grandchildren out of this...so far. If you break our contract, we take more pictures, it's that simple. I'll let you think about it for a couple of minutes."

He clapped Mick on the back and walked off.

"What the fuck is this, Mick?" Keith asked softly, clearly spooked.

"I...don't....really...know," Mick, his voice almost too soft for his partner to hear.

"Are they like William Penn?" Keith, staring at his dead bandmates, absentmindedly playing a riff on his guitar. "Are they preserved and shit but with gears and a metal skeleton or something?"

"Fuck if I know."

"I really don't want to do this, man."

"Neither do I."

But then they thought of their grandchildren and great-grandchildren and walked on stage together. The set list was written on a piece of plexiglass at the front of the stage.

"Start Me Up, what a surprise." Mick, rolling his eyes.

Keith started the song and the other musicians joined in, Ronnie and Charlie included. Only their limbs moved, they were otherwise motionless as they played. Were the robots playing or was it backing tracks? It was impossible to tell. Mick couldn't help but stare at Ronnie who would have normally been mugging and running about.

This has to be Hell. You know, I never looked at what I did in my life as bad, but perhaps I was deluding myself.

And then he was singing Start Me Up for the ten-thousandth time or maybe just the eighth thousandth time. The lights made it difficult to see the audience. It seemed a small place, maybe a few hundred seats. The audience all looked at least in their thirties and mostly white, the people he could see at least. After a couple of songs, Mick got lost in his performance and the next hour and a half passed quickly. He walked off stage without looking at the others, walking briskly back to the dressing room to try and forget where he had been.

5

Fuck you, you bastards.

It was a beautiful selfish act of defiance, very Keith. Mick remembered the day clearly: He had woken up from a backstage dream, pre-show in the dressing room sometime in the 90s. Someone had eaten Keith's shepherd's pie or maybe they had just taken the first slice. The guitarist was roaring around with a fearful assistant by his side---

And then Mick had woken up craving bacon.

I knew something was wrong and that it had to do with Keith...

But what? If he was sick they could cure that. If he was upset, he would mess around with his guitar or do some Carmichael songs on the piano and the mood would pass.

No...it was seismic. Something much bigger than a mood that needed to pass.

He tried to telephone Keith but there was no answer, nothing unusual there. Hati showed up and cooked bacon without being asked to. By that point, Mick was used to having needs or desires met without asking. He didn't eat the bacon. Shortly before noon, there was a message from Turner:

Performances are cancelled for the next two weeks. Will update you when I have new information. Go Team Stones!

Five days later, Turner showed up at the penthouse wearing one of his custom suits and an ingratiating smile.

"How's the world's greatest frontman doing?"

"Dunno, let's call him and ask."

Turner chuckled obligingly and pulled out his phone.

"Hey, I need to show you some pictures, boss."

"I wasn't aware I had done anything to warrant pictures."

They looked at each other. Turner was still smiling but his eyes were cold; the smile reminded Mick uncomfortably of the robots or re-animated corpses or whatever the fuck they were downstairs.

"This has to do with Keith. No one you care for has had pictures taken of them."

Mick wanted to know what Keith had done or what had happened to him and yet he didn't; it had to be awful whatever it was. Every muscle taut, Mick leaned over to stare into Turner's phone. There were grandchildren and great-grandchildren, branded or stabbed or having been tossed off buildings.

"That's the first time you've touched direct family," Mick allowed some rancor into his voice. "You're kind of an asshole, aren't you?"

Turner's smile tightened as he put his phone away.

"Considering how Keith sabotaged the show I consider it warranted."

He pulled out his phone again to show one more picture. Mick winced; he was the last living Rolling Stone.

"So, it goes without saying that all knives will be removed from your kitchen...." Turner said flatly.

"I'm surprised you didn't see that coming."

Turner chucked, clapped Mick on the shoulder, and stood up from the couch.

"It doesn't matter in the end; the show always goes on," his smile became big and happy again. "Always."

Fuck you, you bastards.

Ten days after that, Mick was escorted downstairs for another performance. People---clearly wealthy---would pay unimaginable amounts of money to see the Rolling Stones play an intimate venue. *How much? Hundreds of thousands? Millions? If the news of my "death" is known around the world, what do they think they're seeing? Are they in on my death being faked?*

"Was it fake?" He said that softly, looking over at his kitchen where the knives had been.

Even if there hadn't been knives in the kitchen, Keith always had a couple on him; it was one of his things. Mick imagined Turner realizing what was happening just a few minutes too late, his face morphing in inhuman rage---

Mick saw something awful, what he imagined Turner's real face was like...

A knock on the door: Five minutes until showtime.

This is not the time to think about it. If I am not in peak forms there will be pictures of my great-grandchildren.

When he made his way to the stage, he saw Keith waiting for him. Mick went up as if to touch his old bandmate and Turner's voice came over the house speakers.

"Please, Mick, very delicate machinery."

The singer backed away. It looked like Keith, even smelled like him, but it wasn't him at all, it was just a machine(??) even if it had Keith's skin draped over it. Was it? It looked like Keith skin down to the last splotch and wrinkle. His hair looked exactly the same.

"Amazing work," the singer muttered, nodding a little.

Why do they even bother keeping me alive? Is it because I sing? Couldn't they just have a pre-recorded track or do they at least need me to draw the audience in; one last Stone who can chat and interact with them?

Keith was moving and the riff for Start Me Up was coming over the speakers. The band came in and Mick's hips began moving as if they had a life of their own. He understood that it was just his natural reaction to the music, but what if he tried to remain still? Would they build in something that would allow them to take control of his limbs if he wasn't moving the way they wanted? What if they had *already* built something in?

Mick contemplated standing still to test it, but didn't want to know the truth.

The words started coming out of his mouth as they had thousands of times, hitting the right notes and following the proper rhythm.

255

What if I am just like the others? What if I only think I am different but in reality I am just another robot? What if they transplanted my consciousness into a machine?

He missed a word, Mick had been so caught up in his thoughts he had screwed up a lyric. Maybe an old personal assistant would be mugged or a favorite caterer would break a limb.

He thought of his grandchildren and great-grandchildren and understood that he had to focus on giving another stellar performance.

The show always goes on.

That it did...

in ruhe lassen in ruhe lassen in ruhe lassen in ruhe lassen in ruhe lassen in ruhe lassen in ruhe lassen in ruhe lassen in ruhe lassen in ruhe lassen

Leave in Silence

in ruhe lassen in ruhe lassen in ruhe lassen in ruhe lassen in ruhe lassen in ruhe lassen

in ruhe lassen in ruhe lassen in ruhe lassen in ruhe lassen in ruhe lassen

in ruhe lassen in ruhe lassen in ruhe lassen

What ever happened to Depeche Mode, that promising band that called it a day ten years ago after main man Vince Clarke died? I met with two of the surviving members to get the inside story.

Martin Gore and Dave Gahan are not the fresh-faced young men they were back in 1981. It was early that year when I caught a show at the Hope and Anchor by an up and coming band called Depeche Mode; Martin was the shyest of the three keyboardists on stage and Dave the equally brash and awkward lead singer.

 "Crazy days," Martin chuckles in the present, his teeth charmingly wonky.

Dave appears lost in thought as he takes another long pull off his beer.

"I think about them a lot, maybe too much," he says softly before looking up at me intensely. "We really could have gotten there, you know?"

"We'll never know what could have happened," Martin sighs.

 "I think about it all the time, man." Dave says, lost in his own world, his eyes almost painfully intense. "All the time."

By all accounts Martin avoids Dave. After a few beers his erstwhile partner heads off to the toilets and Martin becomes more forthcoming.

"Dave's an amazing guy," Gore says with a frown. "But he's lost, totally lost now and it's hard to see him like this."

He looks sad and more than a little guilty.

"He's a star and not good at much else," Martin continues softly.

"Dave wanted to carry on after Vince died but I just got a bad taste in my mouth; it felt like God was telling me that being a pop star wasn't the direction I should be going in."

He takes a long drink from his glass before continuing.

"I went back to the bank and they hired me back on and I haven't seen any reason to do anything else."

The former keyboardist pauses and looks in the general direction of the bathrooms.

"Every once in a while I run into Dave and he goes on about how we should get the band back together. The last time I saw him he was in a bad state---I think he'd been huffing because there was blue paint in his stubble---and he told me that he had dreamed we were in a band called A Broken Frame."

Martin stops for a few moments to regain his composure; there is a definite connection between the two men, one complicated by history, broken dreams, and Dave's demons. Andrew Fletcher, a head accountant at a firm in West London, politely declined my interview request. The one rule I was given before speaking to Martin and Dave was that I was not allowed to talk about the 1982 death of Vince Clark. According to a friend of the band, Clark had been attempting to plug a new Synclavier in and there was a fatal electrical mishap. This was a month after the release of the band's second album, *Assembly*. The album had not been far removed from their debut *Speak and Spell* aside from a fine song by Martin (and the last Depeche Mode single), See You. If the senseless death weren't enough, the surviving members of Depeche Mode learned that Vince had been planning to leave the band.

"Supposedly this had been going on with him for some time," Martin frowns again. "He didn't like being a star, didn't like what it involved, and was thinking of becoming a producer or a songwriter; a mutual friend told me he had demoed some stuff for Alf."

Gore picks up on my confusion and continues.

"Alison Moyet, she's supposed to be a great singer, tours in the area with a band...I don't remember the name."

Now Dave has returned and it is Martin's turn to run off and relieve himself. Dave pays me a compliment---something about liking my shirt—and then, still smiling, asks if I can "lend" him the money for another beer. There is a degree of pain in his eyes; beneath the 'Everyone's Buddy/Jack of the Lads' smile there is something tortured and possibly a little off balance.

"This job market is terrible," he shakes his head after I order us another round. "I was working at this greengrocer, doing the stock, you know, but it didn't work out."

I inquired if he was doing anything musical.

"I've tried out for a few bands but nothing ever came of it," Gahan said thoughtfully. "When Depeche Mode ended, Mute offered to have me on as a solo act but that didn't work out."

I want to ask about all the stories of him picking fights with producers and songwriters, of vandalizing the Mute offices and finally being blackballed for being nothing but trouble---

I had planned to ask about those things but there is so much darkness in Dave's eyes and surrounding him that I want to either embrace him and tell him everything will be okay or just run off before he pulls me down.

"You know, the reason Depeche Mode broke up was Fletch," Dave says quietly but with intensity. "I can talk to Mart; he was all in a state when Vince died and told me that it was clear to him that God didn't mean for him to have a career in music. I said, 'No, man, God got us to this point because this is what we should be doing. I can sing and you can write great songs, I mean, See You is fucking incredible, man. One day, he played one called Leave...uh, I think maybe it was Leave in Silence and it was..."

Dave looks away and I wonder if he's crying. When he speaks again, his voice is soft and a weird combination of firm and vulnerable.

"It was beautiful. I had to leave when he played it for me, just walk out, because it made me cry."

He pauses, looks across the room; his upper lip is quivering a bit. When the singer speaks again his voice is a whisper.

"Leave in Silence...I heard Leave in Silence and had to leave in silence."

I asked if he believed Fletch had broken up the band. The vulnerability leaves Dave's face and is replaced by bitterness.

"Yeah, I told Mart, 'We can do this, the three of us—we can get another keyboard player or maybe even a drummer to make things more exciting and he seemed into the idea but then Fletch talked to him and reinforced Mart's whole 'God's will' idea and that was it; because of Fletch Depeche Mode broke up."

Martin has returned to the table but it was a journey of hesitance. I caught sight of him standing across the bar and looking at the table from a distance, watching his old band mate relive the past. Martin looked apprehensive, I could see it from across the room; he appeared to dread coming back to the table and had to will himself to return. Right after he sat down, Dave became more fidgety, looking where a watch had been—("Had to pawn it last week")—and nervously out into the crowd.

"I've got to take off now," he says distractedly. "I have to meet someone."

He looks over at Martin one last time, his gaze openly desperate.

"We should get together sometime and work out some music. I know we could get something great going, Mart. We can do religious songs if you like; call the band Songs of Faith and Devotion or something like that."

Before Gore can respond, Dave gets up and walks away quickly. Martin watches his departure with an alchemy of sadness and relief.

"I tried to get him a job at the bank," Gore says softly. "But he kept coming in late and they had to let him go."

He looks into his pint glass and frowns.

"Coming here was a bad idea," he taps the edge of the glass on the table, seeming to be focused on the contact of glass on wood for a few seconds; a rhythm, the only music he had made in years. "I just can't deal with seeing Dave like this. I run into him every few months; you think of London as a huge city, but in reality it's very small, especially when you frequent the same places as someone you wish to avoid."

He looks up, his face set with guilt.

"Maybe I should put in for a transfer to Liverpool, our bank always has an opening up there. My mum wouldn't like it but it may just make things easier."

der klub

       der klub der klub der klub
der klub der klub der klub der klub der klub der klub der klub der
klub der klub der klub der klub der klub der klub der klub der klub
der klub der klub

       der klub der klub der klub

der klub der klub der klub der klub der klub

The

Club

"I never planned to join that stupid club."

Beck is sitting at a dimly lit back table in the Sheik's Palace, a restaurant that has been open on and off for nearly a hundred years. Back when the gold tape was cut in May, 1923, it was Hollywood's largest and most elaborate restaurant. When I walked in for my interview with legendary singer-songwriter Beck Hansen, however, it was dark and shabby, smelling of old carpet and decades of grease. The musician was sipping water and picking at a plate of chicken and rice. He told me the history of the place, how Harold Lloyd had drunk there and that it was scheduled to be demolished when Jim Carrey hid there for three hours after shooting eleven people a year before our meeting.

"This place is freaky," The songwriter says, looking over at an arched doorway. "That's why I like it."

Beck smiles a little; he seems like a nice guy who is too intelligent to be really nice. Now 53, the lank, blond hair has large samples of silver in it. The light is too poor to make out age lines or the scars from the motorcycle accident that nearly killed him sixteen years earlier. He won't talk about the accident just as he won't talk about Scientology---those are the rules his publicist lays out. When I start talking about Bob Dylan, Beck picks up on the direction I am taking the conversation and, for the only time in our conversation, is curt, shaking his head and gruffly saying, "No. Stop." Maybe a little embarrassed by his own harshness, the singer looks away for a moment. I follow his gaze but it ends at a water stained wall. When Beck speaks again his voice is soft, contrite sounding.

"Sorry, but..." He closes his eyes, sets down his folk. "I never planned to join that stupid club."

It was July of 2007 and he had just returned from a tour of Japan and Australia. *The Information* was proving to be a huge success, selling four million copies worldwide and making Beck Hansen a bonafide star. Since *Odelay*, he had been releasing classic album after classic album culminating with *The Information*. When I am recounting these times I see a smirk reshaping Beck's mouth.

"This is where you write that it was my *Blonde on Blonde*."

"*The Information* wasn't a double album."

"Well, if I had released it in 1966 they probably would have made it a double album."

He picks at his food, taking a small bite and frowning.

"This chicken is a false promise."

While in Australia, Beck and his band had rented motorcycles. The singer loved the experience and bought a new BMW F650CS when he got back home. His wife was less than thrilled but Beck felt that riding would inspire him as other new experiences had inspired him in the past. Instead, it nearly killed him on July 29, 2007.

Reports on the accident are varied:

Some say Beck was speeding, getting in over his head while still a novice rider---an all-too-common story.

Other witnesses claim a car veered into his lane and the singer swerved to avoid it.

More than one witness claimed that he had been run off the road by another motorcyclist, a slender man with curly hair on an ancient Triumph.

Whatever the cause, the end result was Beck breaking his leg and receiving a severe concussion that still gives him headaches. There were also facial lacerations; one "insider" claimed that Beck's face was partially peeled off by the unforgiving pavement when his visor shattered---he certainly looked different in the photos for his next album, *Modern Guilt*. This, of course, led to "Beck is dead" rumors: *He doesn't look the same*, conspiracy theorists claim, *he doesn't sound the same*. According to the conspiracy theories, his manager and record company got a minor league singer-songwriter who looks and sounds like Beck, performed plastic surgery on him, and have had him pretending to be Beck Hansen for the past sixteen years. But what about the new classics? What about the songs that are as good as anything off *The Information* or the classic album *Sorrow's Highway* that came out nine years after the accident? *Recorded before the accident*, the "Beck is Dead" crowd insists: *Beck was very prolific, they just fiddled with the recordings to make it fit in with the other stuff False Beck was doing.*

A few days after my lunch with Beck I met up Marilyn Manson at Perfume in East L.A. A friend of Beck's since a couple of years after the accident, MM is both sympathetic of his fellow musician and understanding of the curiosity surrounding the accident.

"I totally get why these conspiracies exist," Manson says thoughtfully. "How would Beck top *The Information*? How would Dylan have topped *Blonde on Blonde*? Ever since Bob Dylan died in that accident it seems like only a few years passes before some sad wanna be rockstar goes up to New York to re-create the accident in a bid for immortality. One or two times it has worked, most times it doesn't but the formula is always the same: Buy an old Triumph off EBay, take it up to Woodstock to wind it out, and commit two wheel Hari-Kari. It's all so pathetic...I wish I had thought of it."

Had he ever been tempted to do it?

"No, but then again I have too many plans to opt out like that and, to be honest, I was never a fan of Bob Dylan. Of course, you can't say that without people looking at you like you've admitted enjoying the taste of cat shit. I mean, as someone who appreciates rock music I understand those three albums Dylan did in '65 and '66 are classic; he recorded three classic albums and then died tragically at the age of 24. Brilliant, total James Dean move. Of course, I have always understood that even if I took the whole 'death on wheels' option it would only buy me a few years of accolades; my music has never been remotely as good as Dylan's, I get that."

But Beck's music was in the same league, wouldn't he agree?

"*Was?*" Manson looks at me intently. "See, I hear that a lot."

He looks across the room at a fat man in vinyl pants barking like a dog before continuing.

"I think a lot of people were looking to Beck to be our generation's Bob Dylan and consequently die in a motorcycle crash, but he didn't, and consequently he has to pay a big price for surviving."

"Look--here's a picture from around the time that *The Information* was released."

Scott, a bearded and intense young man, is rifling through his Beck collection in his small memorabilia shop located in a strip mall.

"This is classic Beck, as we call him," the shop owner continues, the smell of sweat and grime seeping through his clothes. "Now, here's the cover of *Modern Guilt* from two years later; he looks different just as he sounds different."

And this is proof that Beck died in the motorcycle crash? I ask.

Scott looks at me as if I'm crazy; maybe I am for writing this article.

"No, but it did change him," he says slowly, somewhat patronizingly. "Changed him beyond the obvious disfiguring."

The cover of *Modern Guilt* has Beck grinning, but his smile is as awkward as his stance; maybe it still hurt to stand on the leg that was broken in the accident. Surrounding him are two African musicians and a local woodworker. Legend has it that the faces of the Backstreet Boys were carved into the tree right behind Beck but, the legend continues, the photo was retouched when Kevin Richardson (of the Backstreet Boys) objected.

"The music lost something," Scott continues. "I don't think Beck died in that crash but *something* in him did, maybe the something that made him special. It's like Stevie Wonder's accident---how can one the most brilliant songwriters of the seventies just lose his gift the way Stevie Wonder did in the eighties? With Beck there have been a handful of brilliant songs and *Sorrow's Highway* is an incredible album, but none of it can touch *The Information* or *Sea Change* or even *Guero*."

A teenager with touchingly bad skin walks in and Scott moves behind the counter to watch the young man closely. The kid is drawn to the wall where the most valuable posters hang and appears mesmerized by a poster for Dylan's Highway 61 Revisited.

"How much?" He asks, looking over at Scott.

"Four hundred-fifty, it's an original that Garth Hudson owned, he even wrote a little memorial on the back."

"Garth who?" The kid looks confused.

"He played keyboards in the group that backed up Dylan from time to time."

"Damn, I wish I had the money."

Relaxing, Scott walks over from behind the counter to where the young man is standing.

"I've also got some really good Beck stuff that is a lot more affordable."

The kid looks as if Scott is trying to con him.

"No thanks, man; Beck is a total Dylan wannabe."

Nickels and Dimes

groschen und pfennige groschen und pfennige
groschen und pfennige

groschen und pfennige
groschen und pfennige

1

I have been thinking about telling this story for a while now. The thing is, I have no idea how to approach it:

Do I write it in the third person and pass it off as fiction?

Do I write it in the second person, like someone I know making a confession?

Do I write it in the first person and admit all the terrible things I have done?

This story starts in a house, my mother-in-law's house to be precise. My wife and I had separated and my ex had moved to Kansas City to stay with friends. Having no friends myself I was stuck in that house and, for obvious reasons, felt awkward being there. I was looking for work every day but the job market was in the toilet; there seemed to be no escape from the rooms I stayed in.

My mother-in-law was a hoarder. Every room of that house was full of stuff. When I say "stuff" I mean pretty much whatever you could imagine...*stuff*, lots of it. I kept the rooms I had shared with my ex tidy, but that was like a small oasis compared to the rest of the house. One afternoon the lamp I was using went out. I thought I had spotted some lamps in a downstairs bedroom so I went on a scouting mission. I hated going into those rooms; the whole house was creepy and you could sense all the people who had died within its walls: My ex-wife's father and a couple of siblings were the ones I knew about. I hated opening the bedroom doors and walking in those rooms, *hated* it, but I needed another lamp and didn't have the money to go out and buy one.

I found a lamp in the first room. There was something else in there, something cold that I could feel before I saw it---a huge pile of coins in the middle of the bed, silver ones. I stopped in my tracks and just stared at those coins for what felt like a couple of minutes. Did my mother-in-law even remember they were there? What was the right thing to do in that situation? I knew that if I took them and explained to her what I had done she would be okay with it; she had been very generous with us, very generous with *me*. I was uneasy with the idea of taking those coins but I was broke; after using my Unemployment check to pay my bills I had less than ten dollars to buy groceries.

My mother-in-law would understand, I would just tell her later. I got a canvas shopping bag and went back to that creepy room. There were lots of coins and it took a few minutes to load those nickels and dimes into the bag. I drove over to the nearest grocery store that I knew had a Coinstar machine. Even after paying the fees I had $100, *exactly* $100. There was something creepy about that, something that didn't feel right. I actually walked around the

store for a few minutes wondering if I should just leave that cash on the sidewalk or something---it was that bad of a feeling. After a few minutes of back and forth I decided to keep that $100.
Like I said, I needed groceries.

I bought my groceries and returned to the house. Putting the meat away I noticed a lot of blood in the packaging. The bad feelings returned but at least I had food; life could continue for a few more days. As I lay on the couch reading that night I heard creaking. This was nothing new in that house; you heard creaks, saw shadows, felt people or something watching you. It had seemed like it had been all over the house before but now I understood what room it was coming from.

Every time I walked past the door to the room with the coins I felt something: A chill? A sense of dread or fear? I can't describe it. I knew there was money in there. I knew it was there but I wanted no part of it.
I held out for eight days.

2

Life, as I knew it, continued: I looked for work on all the "career sites." I put in applications with the chain stores and even filled out an application for a burger joint. Nothing: It was brutal out there. Out of the first $100 I had about $30 left---one more trip to the grocery store. And then what? I always had a room at my Mom's down in Lodi but knew she was struggling on her own just like my other family members with spare rooms.

After eight days I returned to the room where I had found the coins; there was a pile of nickels and dimes on the bed just like I knew there would be. They were glittering even though there was very little light in the room. I had brought a canvas bag with me, but I didn't want to touch them.

You need to leave right now. Just leave everything behind and drive to Lodi. Leave this room, leave this house and get away---now.

As you may have guessed, that didn't happen. I stood there for a few minutes more before scooping all of those coins into a bag and making a second trip to Coinstar. The supermarket was busy when I took the coins in. The machine made a hell of a racket as I dropped all of the nickels and dimes in. Shoppers glanced over and probably noticed my worn clothes and troubled expression.

They know you've done something wrong. You need to just leave right now, just leave that dirty money where it is and leave.

But how would I get groceries? How would I live? There wasn't any work out there and my Unemployment had run out. I had $100 in coins in my bag; I could buy some groceries and pay for my Internet so I could keep looking for work. How could I just walk away from that?

When I finished feeding the coins in, I took my receipt up to Customer Service. It was the same girl that had been there the last time I had brought my dirty money in. She was cute and maybe around twenty-five with brown hair and a slim figure.

"Found some more coins, huh?" She was smiling but there was something in her eyes.

What would you expect? You bring all these coins in like a panhandler...or a thief. Do you think any girl in her right mind would have anything to do with you?

"Yeah, just lucky, I guess." I gave her a flirtatious smile but she wasn't having it.

She had already turned to the next customer as she handed me my cash.

My mother-in-law was home when I got back.

"Hey, I got you something from Wendy's on the way home."

I didn't want to take it, didn't want to partake in any more of her kindnesses. How could I tell her about the second trip to Coinstar when I hadn't told her about the first one? Two days. I figured two days was the cut-off after the first trip where I could have come clean about it without looking like a snake.

And now she had bought me food just as she had brought us food on many occasions; small acts of kindness that added up to something so big I knew I could never repay it.

No, you're re-paying it—by stealing from her. Don't you think she could use that money?

I thanked Gracie and asked how she had been but it was all rote and robotic. I didn't want to be there, didn't want to look her in the eye, I felt she could see everything bad rising inside of me. I'm sure she could smell it just like I could smell the food insinuating through the greasy bag.

Going upstairs I closed the door to my room and tore at the food like a beast. Gracie had also bought a case of Budweiser for me so I drank two as I ate---I would drink a total of seven beers that night. There was this undeniable feeling of going down somewhere cool and edged and unpleasant, it was as undeniable as the feeling that I belonged there in such a brutal place.

3

The next few days were so similar they seemed cast in the same mold: I woke up late in the morning, lingered over the computer, ate whatever food was around, and thought about the room. My car insurance would be due at the end of the month; I would need more money—

Don't even think about it.

But did it really matter by that point? I had already taken the money twice, hadn't I already made a pact with whatever was responsible for leaving it there.

What if it was just Gracie testing me? Maybe all the kindness was some sort of head game. Why would anyone be that nice? What was she getting out of it? After all, I was no longer a part of her family, I was the *ex*.

Maybe all of this was some sick game, maybe she had even put cameras in that room so she could observe my trepidation as I debated whether or not to collect the coins...

Maybe she savored those replays like I savored those burgers she had bought me.

Maybe.

But probably not.

After eight days I returned to the room. It smelled like dead blankets and worn carpet and mold. There weren't any coins on the bed, not a single nickel or dime neatly piled on the cheap, floral quilt.

There weren't any coins glinting despite a lack of light.

The canvas bag I had brought would remain empty.

4

A couple of days passed. Normally I can remember my dreams in the morning but for those two days I lost them the moment I opened my eyes. The beer Gracie had bought was nearly gone and most of the Coinstar dollars had been spent. What was I going to do? Gracie had given me carte blanche to raid her kitchen but there was no way I was going to do that. It was part guilt and part self-preservation: Who knew how long that food had been around. I didn't sleep the third night. Part of it was not having any beer to knock myself out with and part was worry: How was I going to eat? How was I going to pay my insurance and my Internet and put fuel in my car?

I drove down to the local music store. The guy who ran it had a suspicious mustache and terrible body odor but it was someplace to kill time. The owner kept asking if I needed help, smiling a grin as yellow as malaria that complimented his cheap, brown slacks. Eventually I had enough of his smiles and smell and fled into the afternoon. I was careless as I backed up and badly scraped the car next to me. I climbed out and inspected the damage: It looked bad, I had really done a number on their car. I went to my glove box to get the number of my insurance agent with the intention of leaving a "sorry about your car" note along with my information.

Wait—is my insurance still valid? Hadn't it been due the day before yesterday? What kind of trouble will I get in for driving a car without insurance? They take your car, don't they?

I glanced around the parking lot, there was no one nearby; I always parked far away from the shops, ironically, to avoid incidents like the one I found myself in. I checked the damage to the car again. It wasn't even a car, it was a newer Lexus SUV; they probably had really good insurance---

They were probably rich and could blow off the deductible like a normal person would blow off the cost of a fast food burger. Aside from the scrape the Lexus was spotless, they probably didn't ever use the four wheel drive just like most people who buy those SUVs. That's why all those people had died in Iraq; all the people in this country who bought SUVs like that Lexus.

I crumbled the note in my hand and climbed in my car.

I started it up and drove back to the house.

5

The Dilapidated Janitor was doing something in the front yard when I got back. He was always puttering on some project, mending a sprinkler line or adding potting soil to some plant or making a walkway. TDJ was Gracie's friend. I don't think he was a boyfriend, more a guy friend or a pal. He was somewhere in his mid-seventies with wonky teeth and a big, white mustache. Like Gracie he was Mexican but unlike her the Janitor didn't really speak English. He seemed okay but Gracie told me he was always trying to boss her around. Maybe it was a cultural thing, *machismo.* Looking back at my car I saw the damage to the fender. Away from the scene of the crime it seemed even bigger than it had been when I first looked at it. I hadn't recalled the Lexus being red---I thought it was a bronze color---but there was a big red mark on the side of my car. The Janitor gave me a misshapen smile and I greeted him in misshapen Spanish.

I felt the house welcome me as I entered the living room. It wasn't the warm sort of welcome you get when you visit a family member or a friend, it felt like the sort of welcome a cat gives a crippled bird; I had fallen and was easy prey. Walking down the dark, narrow hall I didn't have to open the door to the bedroom to confirm there would be a pile of coins on top of the bed. Going up the stairs to my part of the house I could feel whatever was in that room seeping under the door to follow me. I made the last few steps two at a time and slammed my door behind me. It was a night with no beer: I really needed it but I had crushed the last can two nights before. I kept imagining something drifting up the stairs after me and found myself feeling the door for cold spots. That was a ridiculous thought; the entire house was a cold spot.

I waited until late morning before leaving my room. Around eleven the house filled with as much light as it would allow in for the day. I grabbed my canvas sack and headed downstairs. I didn't want to go in that room, knew something bad was in there just biding its time until I came back, but what else could I do? I had nowhere else left to go.

The pile was twice as big as the last time. I could smell the metal of the coins and to me it smelled like blood. Scooping the coins into the bag I felt more and more at ease with each handful. Why had I been scared? Life had been tough the past couple of years; getting a break like this made sense. It was perfectly logical, I belonged in that room...I was meant to be in there.
Once the bag was full I ran out, slammed the door, and swore to myself I would never go back in there.

6

My instincts told me that I couldn't go back to the same Coinstar; that girl seemed to know that something was up. She might have been wearing a fake smile but I could tell that she was on to me; it was time to move on to another supermarket. I was pretty sure there was a Coinstar at the Raley's on Florin.

Driving over I couldn't help but notice all the Lexus SUVs. Isn't it funny how if you're thinking about a car you start seeing them everywhere?
What if one of them was the one I had hit in the parking lot?
What if the driver was some huge guy with a gun or something?
That red mark on the side of my car was hard to miss. Every time I spotted a Lexus SUV I would quickly change my course and speed away, glancing in the rear view mirror to make sure I wasn't being followed.

The Coinstar haul was exactly $200. Exactly. Do nothing, get $100. Fuck up someone's ride get $200...
What if I killed someone?
I was walking out to my car with the cash when I thought that; I shuddered so violently I thought I was going to drop the money---

But, for the sake of argument, *what if?*

And who or what was behind the money? Gracie? No, she would just give me the cash like she had given us cash on countless occasions.

And look at how you've repaid her...

But it was too late to mention the coins now, the betrayal was set in stone. It was bad enough as it was; if I told her it would compound the whole mess by hurting her—

Which brings us back to the big question: Who or what was behind this money?

One thought, and I was pretty sure I didn't want to say the name—*the Devil.*

Even though I hadn't grown up with any sort of religion I still had an awareness and fear of the Devil. Could it be that simple? Could a red guy with a pitchfork be leaving the money behind? Wasn't the Devil supposed to get you to sign something first?

Sorry Mr. Devil, you can't have my soul for those coins; we didn't sign any sort of contract.

It was funny but it wasn't.

I drove over to my insurance office to pay my bill; there were Lexus SUVs in every parking lot and on every street...

How would I explain to Gracie that I was able to buy groceries? I decided that I could tell her that I got a job; I could tell her I got a job and then I could start giving her money—

Money that rightfully belonged to her.

Money that I was still taking from under her roof and had been concealing from her for weeks.

But it'd be something, right? I could kind of repay my debt to her a bit, couldn't I?

What would I have to do to keep the money coming? Putting a gash along someone's car had gotten me twice the amount I had gotten the first couple of times. What if I had set the car alight or made it explode? What if I had smashed into it while it was moving and caused injury to the driver?

I knew the answer, I just didn't want to acknowledge it.

I made a point to listen for when Gracie got home, pulling on a big smile and telling her this big phony story about a temp job I had landed. I had picked up some flowers for her at Raley's and I felt shitty when she almost cried when she saw them; Gracie acted like I was this great guy and it made me feel even worse. I wasn't a great guy; I was a long way from it and getting further away with every bag of nickels and dimes.

7

The next day I didn't even bother looking for jobs online, I was preoccupied with figuring out what I could do to get more coins on that bed without really hurting someone. I didn't have a problem with fucking up some rich guy's SUV or some smug asshole's Toyota Prius. What is it about wanting to save the world that turns people into assholes?

I drove up to McKinley Park to clear my head, just walk around the pond and check out the ducks and geese. There was some large, older woman in an expensive outfit on the path that skirted the water. Instead of taking in what a beautiful day it was she was yakking into her cell phone about how she was fretting that she might only get eight hundred thousand for her house instead of eight and a half. She stopped walking and turned towards the pond. Her back looked as broad as the side of a house and the shadows on the back of her jacket looked like hand prints, *my* hand prints. I glanced around: No one was watching the phone lady, she was just another loud asshole shouting down their mobile phone. I knew what to do and walked forward quickly and without hesitation. The last thing the woman could have expected was someone shoving her from behind; her feet were not planted and she tipped easily over the concrete embankment and into the pond with a big splash.

I had already turned to walk away as I pushed. Not moving hastily, that would allude to guilt, just quickly yet with nonchalance. Still, there was a problem—

She made a big splash and followed it up with some indignant shouting. Even though I was sure no one had been watching us I could have sworn I heard:

"That guy did it! Call the police!"

Maybe one of those good citizens was following me. Maybe they would stay on my trail as I made my way to my car. I glanced over my shoulder a number of times and didn't see anyone but maybe that was the moment they were obscured by a bush or a tree or something. Maybe they would get the plate numbers on my car—

Maybe they see the rear fender of my car was covered with another car's paint and report that as well.

I got in my car and drove away. Passing a Lexus SUV on the other side of the street I saw the driver scowling at me.

Pulling up to the house I saw the Janitor's car parked nearby. It was an ancient Chevy the size of a school that had been kept running with baling wire and chewing gum since Mexico was a Spanish colony. He grinned his haphazard grin and sputtered something in English so broken I felt compelled to rummage in my pockets for Krazy Glue. The Janitor sighed, muttered some fatalism in Spanish, and then returned to his car for something.

The house was still cluttered, but I didn't feel the dread going into it I had felt previously; I knew what was waiting for me in the bedroom. I did not stop at that point in the hall and walk in. Regarding the woman in the park I vascillated between "I hope she wasn't hurt!" to "Fuck that noisy asshole!" I fretted that she may have twisted or even broken something falling into the pond. She couldn't have drowned; it was only a couple of feet deep. Maybe if she had hit her head and been knocked out but I had heard her thrashing in the water as I walked away.

Once upstairs I got on my computer and checked the news. A group in Sacramento had been emulating the Occupy Wall Street movement but had been making little impact. Occupy Sacramento seemed a bit limp, a bit unfocused. It was too bad because I believed in what they were doing—
Maybe I should fuck up a bank. Maybe I should burn down a Wells Fargo or a Bank of America or a Chase.
Okay, believing in something is one thing but—
Maybe the entity that left the coins in the room wouldn't see that as an act of evil, maybe they would see it as "good" and then there wouldn't be a payoff but—
Maybe it seemed like a good thing to do just for the sake of doing it.
That said, how do you destroy a bank? I mean, for one thing most of them are in areas with a lot of foot traffic. For another, there are

lots of cameras around them. Lastly, arson is not a simple matter:
Have you seen CSI? If a pubic hair drops down your pant leg
during the crime they can catch you. They show up, run some crazy
tests, and haul you off to jail.

It took me three days to figure out how to pull it off.

I won't bore you with the details of how I destroyed the Bank of
America on Alhambra. It took a week of planning and practicing
but in the end it burned and I got away. Doing something like that
is weird because at first you are terrified, terrified enough to throw
up as I did, but when you hear the windows blow out and feel a new
heat coloring the night it is like everything you ever imagined
possible in life expands, blooms with color, and fills your blood
with a sort of charge that makes you feel like you could run a
thousand miles.

I watched people stare at the fire, taking in its magic. Some hippy
guy threw a brick or rock at the burning building.

"Fuck the man!" He shrieked.

A cop car pulled up followed by another. Cops jumped out and
grabbed the hippy; that was my cue to leave.

Driving back to the house I imagined coins overflowing the bed; I
would probably use every canvas shopping bag I owned and would
have to map out all the Coinstar locations in the Sacramento area.

Going in the house I didn't notice all the clutter or feel the shadows judging my every step; that fire had to have gotten me hundreds of dollars—

I stopped at the bedroom door.

Something was telling me that the bed would be coin free---

I didn't have to open the door and look inside to understand that; in my heart I saw the bareness of the cheap, floral throw.

"It has to affect a person," I whispered to myself. "A bank is not a person."

Halfway up the stairs I stopped and looked back down the dim hallway. Wait---people *were* affected. What about the tellers who would miss work while they rebuilt the bank? Feeling hopeful I ran down to the bedroom, threw open the door, and flicked on the light.

The top of the bed was bare.

Opening Facebook I checked out the Occupy Sacramento site. It was abuzz with the news of the bank being torched and about how the police roughed up the hippy that had thrown something at the fire. People were outraged; they didn't see some stupid hippy that had made himself look guilty of setting the fire, they saw the police brutalizing a peer....

They saw it as the police standing on the side of a big bank. Before they had been passive and non violent but I had the feeling that was going to change.

9

The next morning I took a shit and scooped it into a gallon sized Ziploc; it was easily the most disgusting thing I have ever done but I had a plan.

Wearing a Raiders cap and a fake mustache I had bought at the costume shop, I parked my car half a mile from Arden Faire mall and walked up to the shopping center using back streets. In the Ziploc I had also poured some lighter fluid that I had found in the storage room downstairs. Prowling the edge of the parking lot, I came across a Hummer H2 that was at least a couple hundred feet from people walking to or from their cars. My hands started shaking badly—would I be able to manage my task? I *had* to. I broke one of the Hummer's side windows with a brick. As I had expected the car had an alarm and the sound was deafening even wearing earplugs. I shattered the window with my left hand and dropped the brick inside. The next step was opening the Ziploc and pouring the contents on the backseat of that SUV. The smell was amazing; I could see waves coming off it and struggled not to throw up as I was overwhelmed by the stench of feces and fuel. The last part of the puzzle was a box of kitchen matches I had filled with torn up newspaper to keep the handful of matches company. I lit a match, put it inside the box, and tossed it through the window. It landed in the middle of the mess. By that point I was shaking so bad my teeth were chattering. I wanted to run but knew that the best thing was to walk away quickly but calmly. Had anyone been drawn by the noise? Apparently not; it was just another car alarm. People were walking up the aisle towards the H2 but they didn't look curious or concerned. I walked right across their line of sight and kept going, the backpack in my gloved right hand. When I was a few hundred feet away I heard a commotion, people yelling in surprise; it was hard not to look back but I had to keep moving. I tore the cap and mustache off and shoved them in the bag. I shifted the bag from hand to hand as I took off the jacket I had bought at a Goodwill the day before. At the edge of the parking lot I glanced over my shoulder and saw tendrils of smoke in the general area where the H2 was parked.

Seeing a trash can I did a quick check of my surroundings; there were people nearby so I kept moving until I found a bin with no one around. Then and only then I dropped the backpack in the bin without slowing my pace.

I would burn the gloves once safely at home.

10

There was three hundred dollars on the bed when I got back to the house. I closed the door behind me and just stared at all those nickels and dimes for a couple of minutes.

"You liked that, didn't you?" I asked softly.

Of course it did, what I had done to that SUV was *inspired.* I filled my canvas bag and enjoyed how heavy it felt. Maybe I would take it to the first Coinstar I had used even if that snooty girl with the fake smile was there. Fuck her---yeah, I was cashing in coins for money but at least I was doing something with my life, I wasn't in some dead end customer service job where I had to smile at people I wished would crawl off and die. Not me; I had a fun, creative job with limitless possibilities.

The fires were all over the local news; I had become a local celebrity even if no one knew my name. On one channel the Fire Chief was mumbling under his mustache that the person who had firebombed the Bank of America and the H2 at Arden Faire would be caught.

Sure...you keep telling yourself that.

The Fire Chief went on to state that he did not believe the crimes were connected but that it was too early in the investigation to tell.

Even though I had been careful I could smell lighter fluid on my pants. Weird, I had been naked when I poured the fuel in the Ziploc and that Ziplock had been in another plastic bag but stranger things have happened. Maybe when I had been pouring the contents of the bag into the H2 my pants had soaked up the fumes or something.

The next day I worked on sanding off some of the red paint on my car; I kept seeing the paint so I sanded down to bare metal.

"You didn't have work today?"

Shit, Gracie---I forget she doesn't work on Wednesday.

"No, my assignment ended but they said they should find me something in a week or so."

I forced a reassuring smile. Gracie walked over and put a twenty dollar bill in my hand which didn't make me feel any less lousy. I thanked her but she was preoccupied with the fender of my car.

"I still think you should have called the police," she said.

"Ah, it's too late for that."

"Did you call your insurance agent?"

"Yes. My deductible for this sort of thing is $500 so I am going to have to save up before I can fix it."

She nodded and fortunately changed the subject. I had told her that someone had clipped my car when I had been in the CVS the day after I had backed into that Lexus. Gracie seemed to buy my story and it made me feel like an even bigger creep. How many more lies was I planning on telling her? The worst thing was that our strange relationship would be continuing for some time: I couldn't move out, if I did, how could I collect the coins? I knew her schedule so in theory I could wait until she was gone and then sneak in but when she wasn't around the Janitor seemed to be on the scene and he would probably gossiped to her about everything I was doing. Worse, if I was gone for a couple of days I risked Gracie finding the coins herself. What would she do if she found them? I mean, I had no problem with a couple hundred dollars going her way, I owed it to her tenfold, but what if she did something unexpected like putting a lock on that bedroom door or something?

No, I had to stay close and make sure nothing happened to my coins.

11

I was trying to keep as little cash in my account as possible; my ex and I had been unable to pay on our credit cards for years and I understood that it was a matter of time before our creditors caught up with me. I also believed it would look suspicious if I was putting hundreds of dollars in cash in my account every couple of days. My plan was to keep the cash there, in the house, probably in a fireproof safe that I needed to buy. My ex-wife had left most of her stuff in the other room; I could hide the safe behind all the boxes and bags.

I spent a couple of hours that night researching safes and found I could get one for about a hundred dollars. I spent the rest of my waking hours *thinking*, trying to come up with more ways to get nickels and dimes that wouldn't actually hurt anyone, not permanently, at least. I hadn't maimed or killed anyone and meant to keep it that way.

What about the woman you pushed into the pond? You don't think she got bruised and scratched up? Plus, she was kind of old and overweight—what if she had a heart attack?

Bullshit; I heard her screaming and thrashing in the water.

And she wouldn't be doing that if she was having a coronary? If you suddenly had intense chest pains wouldn't you be thrashing around?

Chances are you killed her—chances are you took her life for a bunch of nickels and dimes.

No, that was just the guilt talking. I mean, I had good reason to feel guilty, I had done some bad stuff, but I hadn't killed anyone....I was nearly certain of that,

The next morning I planned my day out as I dressed. Even though I put on clean pants I could still smell lighter fluid—had I spilled some in the bathroom? Even after scrubbing the floor for about twenty minutes I could still smell it; I would need to pick up some stronger cleaner when I was out.

Gracie was repotting some plants in the front yard. I put the bags of coins in my car and then walked over for the required small talk; I didn't want to chat but I owed her a hello—
No, I owed her a lot more than that.
"There are a lot of police cars out today." She said.
"Really?"
"Yes, I heard some of the protestors set a police truck on fire and the police have been working to keep the city secure."
"I wonder why they set a police truck on fire?"
I asked that even though I knew the answer: It had all started when that hippy was arrested when the Bank of America was firebombed. It had all started with *me*; I had indirectly caused the riots and burned that police truck.

I had no idea how to feel about that.

My biggest concern was taking care of business; getting that safe and figuring out new ways to get more coins.

After saying goodbye I walked back to my car and saw traces of red paint on the fender---I thought I had gotten all that paint off.

As the car warmed up I added fine sandpaper to my shopping list.

12

There *were* a lot of cops on the streets: Lots of patrol cars, a couple of SWAT trucks, and a few paddy wagons. I doubted they would be able to connect my trips to Coinstar with the fires but I had to assume they would be able to make that connection if I made the *smallest* mistake.

I saw some college-aged kids in a Subaru wagon with "99%" haphazardly written on the sides; they had the windows down and were yelling slogans; two patrol cars appeared out of nowhere and forced those kids off the road.

I hit two different Coinstars in Citrus Heights and Folsom and then went by a Lowes for my little safe. I still had some extra cash in my pocket so I stopped for a big cheeseburger at In 'n' Out and watched the traffic as I ate it. There had been something satisfying about fucking up that Hummer the day before. In my mind I could see some rich guy walking out to his ride pushing a cart with hundreds of dollars worth of stuff in it. As he crossed the parking lot his beaming "got the world on a string" expression would morph into a mask of anger and disgust.

I wanted to do the same thing to an Escalade or maybe one of those Volvo SUVs---for some reason the idea of a Volvo SUV really pissed me off.

Logically, all the malls would be alerted to my activity and would have extra patrols out and more cameras being installed. How long would it take to get those cameras up? They had probably made it a high priority so I had to assume they'd get them up within 24 hours. Hitting another shopping mall would be risky, I would have to take my business elsewhere.

Driving back I took a side trip to the Whole Foods on Arden Way; you can always find entitled assholes at the Whole Foods. After a couple of minutes, I came across some upmarket guy in his fifties sauntering through the wine section with his nose in the air. He was on his mobile phone having a conversation about skiing and the poor service at various resorts and didn't even see me or the pen knife in my hand; I stuck that knife in and twisted it creating a hole in a plastic bottle of canola oil, the cooking oil burbling out as I pretended to peruse some expensive Pinot Noir. The man changed subjects from ski resorts to good places to berth sailboats in the Bay Area. The world around him continued not to exist including the cooking oil he was about to walk through. As he realized that, yes, his feet were moving in a fashion he could have neither predicted nor control, the change in facial expression was priceless; it went from "got the world on a string" to "Oh fuck—I am going down." The bodily motions that followed were a work of art, changing from a school of smug realism to an abstract, all flailing limbs and twisted torsos Picasso homage. He went down with a crunch and his face instantly went red and twisted in pain. In an instant, it went from a fun prank that would hopefully get me more coins to something very different.

Had I gone too far?

That had been a bad crunching sound—had he fractured something? What if he'd never walk right again?

It's too late for growing a conscience. You need to get out—-now.

I set the basket with the leaking oil container down and looked around as if seeking help. I went into Good Samaritan mode and walked over to Customer Service.

"Hey, you need to call 911! Some guy in the wine section fell down, I think he's hurt!"

Before the soft looking guy with the ginger beard behind the counter responded I was walking towards the exit. On the way out to my car I had a bad realization.

What if that guy sues? An asshole like that probably has his lawyer on speed-dial. What if he sues and the store does a full investigation of the incident including reviewing the security footage? How many times do you think they'd have to review the tape before picking out you doing something to that bottle of oil?

But I had been subtle. It was a small gesture and the pen knife was mostly palmed. Besides, I didn't have a record; they would have no idea how to find me—

Unless they have already made a composite from the Bank of America security footage and the footage from the Arden Faire parking lot and the witness descriptions from when you pushed that lady in the pond. You know *someone saw, you* know *that you heard "That guy did it!"*

It's just a matter of time before they catch you.

The worry was making my hands shake as I unlocked my car.

There was a Lexus SUV parked on the next aisle with the hatch up as groceries were loaded in; the driver stopped what she was doing to turn and stare at me.

13

I took the surface streets home. Passing Sacramento State, I saw students demonstrating out front. It wasn't the placid sign waving and chanting of a few weeks earlier, I could feel the rage radiating out from them in waves which felt warm but with the pulsing sting of an electrical shock. The cops were surrounding the protestors with riot shields. I was curious what would happen but traffic moved on before I had a chance to see.

There was a cop car a few cars behind me as I drove down J Street. I ran the inventory all of us run when we see a cop car: Am I speeding? Are my lights working? Have I done anything stupid in the past couple of minutes?

It was just a matter of time. You know they got you on camera throwing that backpack away and all the other cameras will tie you to torching that Hummer. They already have your prints on file—remember when you became a Notary Public a few years ago? You're in the System, they know who you are.

I turned on a side street so I could drive slower and focus on my breathing, focus on suppressing the panic that was setting in. I just had to pull off the street and take a few minutes to get it together— The cop car turned down the same street. Fuck me.

OK, I just had to be calm, it could be a coincidence; I just needed to drive a safe speed but not too slow, obey all the traffic signs, and make the next turn.

The cop car followed me down that street as well and had closed the distance. *Oh fucking hell.*

When the lights came on I thought I was going to piss myself. Scratch that—I thought I was going to *shit* myself.

I pulled over and was shaking so badly I could barely shift the car into park. I had to be radiating guilt, I knew I was so freaked out they would *know* that I had done something wrong. I knew—

And then this peculiar calm feeling swept over me from my head to my toes and to the tips of my fingers. Although it reassured me and stopped my shaking I had the undeniable sensation I was being *invaded*—that I was being *possessed.*

You're panicking over nothing. You wore gloves at the Bank and America and at Arden Faire. Do you think they could make a visual ID by this point? And they wouldn't be apprehending you this way—they would get a warrant and show up at Gracie's house.

I kept both hands on the wheel. One cop stayed in the car and the other walked up to my passenger window and tapped on it.

"The window is broken, officer; open the door if you want."

He did and asked for my license and registration.

"Do you know why I am pulling you over today, sir?"

"No—was I speeding?"

"No...your car fits a profile—"

And whatever had possessed me was gone—*oh shit, oh fucking shit!*

"—we're pulling over old diesels like this one."

"Really?" One word was all I could manage without croaking or stuttering.

"Cars like this tend to be owned by people in fringe groups with anti-government agendas. We have been given instructions to pull these sort of cars over and make a few inquiries. Do you happen to belong to any such groups, sir?"

"Uh, no."

"We will be running your name and accessing your Internet records and if we find anything, it would be better for all of us if you were open and honest with us at this time, sir."

"I get my news from sources other than the mainstream media, is that what you mean, officer?"

"No, sir. We mean being registered on extremist sites and frequenting those sites on a regular basis. Are you registered on any such sites, sir?"

"No, officer; not me."

A tight smile turned up his mustache a bit.

"Very good, sir. Have a nice day."

I managed a feeble smile and a nod, my hands still clutching the steering wheel. I couldn't let go even after they had driven away. I just clutched that wheel as if it was all keeping me tethered to reality.

14

The next thing I was aware of was sitting in Gracie's driveway with the motor still running. I did not remember driving there after the cops pulled me over. I want to say I saw the police setting a checkpoint over on Broadway, but that could have been my imagination. Locking the car, I looked around for Gracie's ancient Dodge Aspen but she must have still been at work. The keys felt cold in my hand and I didn't want to go in that house. What had happened? I had felt at ease there the past couple of days, felt safe, but that afternoon my instincts were telling me to get in my car and drive away.

The lady you pushed in the pond is in there. She is in one of the bedrooms sitting on the bed and thinking about what you did to her, how you killed her.

I forced myself to unlock the front gate. That lock was stubborn and sometimes required a couple of minutes jiggling to get it unlatched. It was one thing when you were going *in*—
But when you were trying to leave it could be unnerving.
Sometimes walking down the hall past all those bedrooms it felt like something was coming to life inside them; reaching up to open the doorknobs and maybe stop you before you got outside---
When you were trying to leave it could feel like a lifetime before you got the door unlocked.

I was all too aware of an absence of light in the living room that afternoon. All the blinds were kept closed; it was always heavy with shadows even in midday. Most times I was only slightly aware of it, but that afternoon I made a connection that I had avoided making in the past—it was like entering a tomb.

I went down the hall to the bedroom. Looking at the pile of nickels and dimes on the bed I guessed there was about two hundred dollars there. I scooped the coins into a bag and walked out of the bedroom. Out of the corner of my eye I noticed the doorway to the back bedroom was cracked. It wasn't opened wide like Gracie opened the doors when airing out the bedrooms, it just cracked. She never cracked doors; they were either wide open or tightly shut—someone or something had to have opened that door. In the past I had used that room for exercising but had gotten spooked when I could have sworn I saw the closet door opening. I ran out of that room and had not been back since; I had closed the door tightly, though, I remember that for sure.
Now it was open a crack—like when you crack your door to spy on your neighbors.
I ran up the stairs two at a time and locked the door to my room. What was going on? I thought whatever left the coins and I had an arrangement; I conducted some business and it left coins on the bed. It was a simple arrangement but a good one—what had

happened? That feeling of being watched was back along with the sensation of weighted darkness---

The big cold spot was back.

I kept seeing the door to the back bedroom cracked open like something was watching me. I was not looking forward to sleep as I was certain my dreams would not be good ones.

15

Where would I conduct my business? I was guessing that I could hit the Coinstars I had used in the past; no one would probably remember me, they had to get hundreds if not thousands of customers every day—

You keep telling yourself that.

The snooty clerk wasn't there. Her place had been taken by some black woman as wide as she was tall with a strange birthmark on her neck. She didn't pass judgment, didn't speak aside from the bare minimum; her essence had already been carried up to the mothership like the colonists at Roanoke or those girls at Hanging Rock. Maybe twenty feet away, though, a middle-aged man with an angry red mustache was staring at me. I am guessing he was a store manager because he was wearing a cheap, white button down shirt and striped tie.

He recognizes you. You've been here three times with hundreds of dollars in nickels and dimes—don't you think that is a little suspicious? He will call the police after you leave. They will review the security footage and compare it to the composite drawing from the witnesses at the pond and the Whole Foods and then match it to your fingerprints. Won't be long now.

The traffic felt weird driving back to Gracie's house. I had another bit of business in mind but something about the traffic had me fearing any detours. I could swear I could hear sirens wailing in the distance but maybe it was in my head. I needed a beer--it wasn't even noon but I desperately needed a drink.

There was a checkpoint on Broadway near Alhambra but I spotted it from a couple of blocks away and turned onto a side street. *They're watching all approaching traffic. The way an old Mercedes diesel looks and sounds stands out, they will probably send a car to intercept you...*
But none came. The rest of the drive home was smooth. *Was* it my home? I guess it was whether I wanted it to be or not. The key in the front gate turned a little too smoothly. I couldn't feel anything and it made me suspicious: I always felt *something* in that house; if it wasn't unease it was a touch of darkness.
There wasn't anything, the house was becalmed. Even the door to the back bedroom was closed—who had closed it? Gracie? Someone else? The strangest thing was my own frame of mind: I felt calm and at peace, like I hadn't a single worry in the world. Everything made sense...I didn't even run up the stairs.

Back in my room I grabbed a beer and sat on the couch. As I opened the can I heard what sounded like mortar fire followed by an air raid siren in the distance. Smelling smoke, I looked out the window but only saw the trees surrounding the yard. I took another sip of beer and watched a squirrel dart through the branches. I finished the can, dropped it in the recycling bin, and got the notebook I used for jotting down ideas.

I needed to get back to business...

All stories written between 2010 and 2021 in:

Phoenix, Arizona

Lodi and Sacramento, California

Fernley, Nevada

Portland, Oregon

And an equipment shed in the middle of the Deschutes National

Forest (Oregon)

www.ingramcontent.com/pod-product-compliance
Lightning Source LLC
Chambersburg PA
CBHW070737180626
46818CB00007B/2881